SPECIAL MESSAGE TO READERS

This book is published under the auspices of

THE ULVERSCROFT FOUNDATION
(registered charity No. 264873 UK)

Established in 1972 to provide funds for research, diagnosis and treatment of eye diseases. Examples of contributions made are: —

A Children's Assessment Unit at Moorfield's Hospital, London.

•

Twin operating theatres at the Western Ophthalmic Hospital, London.

•

A Chair of Ophthalmology at the Royal Australian College of Ophthalmologists.

•

The Ulverscroft Children's Eye Unit at the Great Ormond Street Hospital For Sick Children, London.

You can help further the work of the Foundation by making a donation or leaving a legacy. Every contribution, no matter how small, is received with gratitude. Please write for details to:

THE ULVERSCROFT FOUNDATION,
The Green, Bradgate Road, Anstey,
Leicester LE7 7FU, England.
Telephone: (0116) 236 4325

In Australia write to:
THE ULVERSCROFT FOUNDATION,
c/o The Royal Australian and New Zealand
College of Ophthalmologists,
94-98, Chalmers Street, Surry Hills,
N.S.W. 2010, Australia

A TENDER TRAIL

When Quinn Quartermain saved teenager April St. Clair from a dangerous situation, she fell in love with her handsome rescuer, yet never expected to see him again . . . Years later Quinn, a victim of amnesia, appears on her doorstep needing sanctuary from reporters. They are hounding him for details of a tragic accident of which he has no recall. To April, helping Quinn is merely returning a kindness — a teenage crush couldn't develop into an everlasting kind of love . . . could it?

MOYRA TARLING

A TENDER
TRAIL

Complete and Unabridged

LINFORD
Leicester

First published in the
United States of America in 1987

First Linford Edition
published 2010

All the characters in this book are fictitious. Any
resemblance to actual persons, living or dead,
is purely coincidental.

British Library CIP Data

Tarling, Moyra.
   A tender trail. - - (Linford romance library)
   1. Love stories
   2. Large type books
   I. Title II. Series
   823.9'2–dc22

   ISBN 978–1–44480–227–6

Published by
F. A. Thorpe (Publishing)
Anstey, Leicestershire

Set by Words & Graphics Ltd.
Anstey, Leicestershire
Printed and bound in Great Britain by
T. J. International Ltd., Padstow, Cornwall

This book is printed on acid-free paper

To my family with love

To Bernice and Bertha
with gratitude

Prologue

Quinn lay on the bed, staring at the clean white plaster cast that encircled his thumb and the lower part of his right arm. Once again anger and frustration began to well up inside him. Why couldn't he remember what happened?

He leaned back and closed his eyes, shutting out the peaceful familiarity of his bedroom. He'd thought that once he was back in his own home his memory would return, and the questions that had been plaguing him since he woke up in the hospital three days ago would all be answered.

How stupidly naive those hopes had been. He remembered nothing, had no recollection of the crash, no memory of the hours preceding the accident that had taken Sasha's life, robbing the world of a talent as yet untapped. The

1

only memory Quinn had was the sound of her voice screaming his name.

What had happened? How had they come to be driving around Los Angeles at three in the morning? The questions surfaced once more, accompanied now by a throbbing ache in his head.

Perspiration beaded his forehead and he closed his eyes, trying desperately to unlock the mystery of those missing hours. His head was aching fiercely now, as it always did each time he tried to force himself to remember.

He felt a hand touch his shoulder and he opened his eyes. His longtime friend Ian McKenzie stood by his bedside, an anxious expression on his face.

'Are you all right, Quinn?'

'No, dammit, I'm not all right.' Quinn's voice was edged with anger. 'God help me, Ian! Why can't I remember what happened?'

'Take it easy, buddy,' Ian said soothingly. 'Give it time. That's what the doctors said, wasn't it?'

'Yes,' Quinn agreed with a sigh, 'but I can't shake the feeling that something's not right.' His left hand traced a path through his hair.

'What makes you think that?' Ian asked with a puzzled frown.

'It's just a feeling. I can't explain it. I know the police are satisfied it was an accident, but I just wish I could remember exactly what happened. And now the press are after me to make a statement . . . How can I, when I don't remember a thing about the accident? All I remember is Sasha screaming my name . . . ' His words trailed off, pain evident in his tone.

'Don't do this to yourself, Quinn,' Ian said quickly, seeing his friend's distress. 'Didn't Dr. Cassidy assure you that your memory will return one day, and soon? Just don't push it. Give it time. What you need is to get away for a few days, maybe a few weeks. It'll give you a chance to recover from the trauma of the accident.'

Quinn eased himself off the bed and

moved to the window, where he stood for a long moment staring out at the night. Darkness was steadily creeping over the city, but Quinn could easily discern the small huddle of reporters who had camped out at the foot of his driveway. He turned back into the room.

'And just where would you suggest I go? The minute I set foot outside the front door, those reporters will be all over me.'

'Then we'll just have to figure a way to get you out of here without anyone knowing you've gone,' Ian said calmly.

Quinn studied his friend. 'I can tell that you have something in mind,' Quinn said ruefully. 'Come on, out with it. I want to hear your hair-brained scheme before I agree to it, though this is one time my options are somewhat limited.'

'Trust me. This one's a winner,' Ian assured his friend. 'I just have to make a quick telephone call and we'll be in business. In the meantime, get Robson to pack a suitcase for you and tell him that for the next few days he'll have to pretend to everyone that you're confined to bed and not giving interviews. By then we should be well on our way.'

'On our way where?' Quinn asked, his dark eyebrows rising questioningly.

'You'll see,' Ian said, quickly making his exit and leaving Quinn staring after him in bewilderment.

1

April sat in the old rocking chair on the patio of the cabin huddled in her warm ski jacket, staring at the stars. All she could hear was the quiet lap of water as the sea gently caressed the shore and the melodic jingle of the wind chimes above her head as they moved in the breeze.

She'd forgotten how peaceful and serene this tiny corner of the world always seemed to be. Sitting in the quiet solitude and breathing in the tangy sea air, she realized just how much she'd missed her home in the small resort town of Birch Bay on Washington's coast.

For the past two years she'd been living and working in Seattle where she and her friend, Bobbi Chantel, ran a bridal boutique. Only that morning, April had been putting the finishing touches to a wedding gown she had designed.

Now, as she watched the moonlight dance on the waters of the bay, a feeling of contentment stole over her. For the first time in weeks she allowed herself the luxury of simply doing nothing.

Leaning back in the battered old rocker, she dug her hands deeper into the pockets of her jacket, enjoying this feeling of utter contentment. For the past three months she and Bobbi had been working almost day and night on the gowns for Teresa Santini's wedding. There were six bridesmaids, two flower girls and, of course, the bride herself. The wedding was a monumental task, especially when each dress required additional hand sewing. But they had done it. They had successfully completed the labor of love and now all that remained was the final fitting in a little less than a week.

The timing had worked out perfectly. Well, nearly perfectly, thought April, recalling her mother's rather frantic telephone call to the boutique earlier that morning.

April's mother was flying to New Zealand later that evening to visit her twin sister, whom she hadn't seen in eight years. Laura St. Clair's three-week trip had been planned for months. So, too, had been the arrangements for April to return home to keep an eye on her fourteen-year-old brother, Greg. April had assured her mother everything was under control and that she would be on her way home in a matter of hours.

Needless to say, the next few hours passed rather feverishly for both April and her mother, with time only for another brief call to say goodbye. By midafternoon, April was on her way to Birch Bay.

Now she sat staring into the darkness, watching the odd flash of silvery white as a wave broke the surface of the water, and her thoughts turned to Greg. She knew her mother was worried about him. He'd been having some problems at school lately, but when he'd been asked about them, he'd simply shrugged his shoulders and said nothing.

April tried to tell her mother that most teenagers were under a great deal of pressure and that Greg would sort things out on his own. But because she knew her mother would continue to fret, April had promised to try and find out what was troubling him. Even though she was twelve years older than Greg, they'd always shared a special closeness; perhaps he'd be more willing to talk to her.

Thinking back to her own teenage years, she could recall some of the problems she'd faced. They'd seemed insurmountable at the time, but she'd survived. Greg was levelheaded — he'd make it, too.

Sighing, she tried to bury herself deeper in the folds of her jacket. The chilly November night air was steadily seeping into her bones, but she continued to sit outside, savoring the peacefulness. The muffled sound of the telephone ringing in the cabin suddenly broke the stillness. Reluctantly April rose from the rocking chair to answer it.

'Hello.'

'Laura?'

'No, I'm sorry, she isn't here right now. May I help you?' April asked, changing the telephone receiver from one hand to the other as she slipped off her jacket and dropped it on the chair.

'Ian McKenzie here — '

'Ian! It's April. How are you?' April greeted her cousin enthusiastically. It had been months since she'd talked to Ian or his wife Jane.

'April! I didn't expect to find you there. Home for the weekend?'

'Well, no, not exactly,' April said. 'I'm here for the next three weeks. Mother's off to New Zealand to visit Aunt Frances.'

'Of course. I'd forgotten about that. Damn! I was going to ask your mother a favor,' Ian said, his tone suddenly serious. 'I'll just have to ask you instead.'

'Shoot,' April said as she dropped into the armchair by the telephone.

'Do you remember my friend Quinn Quartermain? You met him briefly at my wedding, I believe. He's been in the news rather a lot lately — I'm sure you've noticed.'

At the mention of Quinn's name, April experienced a brief quickening of her pulse, which she immediately rationalized as a reaction countless women would have.

'Yes, I have,' she admitted.

'The favor I want to ask concerns him,' Ian said.

'I don't understand — ' April began, but Ian hurried on.

'I'm with Quinn now. I drove him home from the hospital a couple of hours ago. To tell you the truth, he's not in good shape, mentally or physically. What he needs is to get out of L.A., away from all this media attention to some quiet out-of-the-way place where he can recuperate.'

'You mean here?' April's heart skidded to a halt . . . then galloped off once more.

'Exactly. Birch Bay would be an ideal spot. Who would ever think of looking for him there? What do you say? Could he hole up in one of the beach cabins for a while?'

April hesitated. She had no difficulty recalling the news reports she'd heard and read during the past few days. The attention Quinn Quartermain had been getting recently was a far cry from the kind of coverage he normally received. She felt saddened by this treatment of a man she had always admired. Sasha Gray's death was a tragic loss — she was a beautiful and talented actress — but the fact that Quinn had suffered a broken wrist and a concussion in the accident seemed to have been overlooked. And if the newspaper reports prior to the accident were to be believed, Quinn's personal loss was infinitely more devastating — he had lost the woman he loved.

'I'd like to help,' April said slowly, 'but the cabins are boarded up during the winter months.'

'So much for my brilliant idea,' Ian replied, disappointment evident in his tone. 'I hate to see Quinn in such pain, and now the reporters have set up camp outside his house. They've been patient so far, but I don't think they're going to leave him alone until they get what they want — an interview.'

April's heart contracted in sympathy. How could she refuse to help Quinn? Ten years ago he had rescued her from a rather dangerous situation. She shivered at the memory.

'I suppose he could stay here with us . . . ' April heard herself say.

'Do you mean it, April? Are you sure?' Ian asked eagerly.

'If you don't think he'd mind,' she answered. 'The guest room isn't very big, but it does have an adjoining bathroom.'

'I really appreciate this, April. You're

a life-saver — I mean that,' Ian said in heartfelt tones. 'Now if the second step of my plan succeeds, we're in business.'

'This is beginning to sound like something out of a spy thriller,' April commented. 'Just how do you propose to get him here without anyone recognizing him?'

'Good question,' came the reply. 'I think we'll have to forget the airport. Someone is sure to spot him. And he's in no condition to drive himself anywhere.' Ian seemed almost to be thinking aloud. 'It's beginning to look like I'll be paying you a visit, too.' He laughed.

Ian rang off at last. As April slowly replaced the receiver, she found herself wondering if Quinn would remember her. Perhaps his memory of that evening had faded; after all it had been ten years ago. But April knew that the memory would stay with her forever, for Quinn's timely arrival in the hotel's underground garage that night had saved her from a disastrous situation.

And now they would meet again. The thought sent a shiver of anticipation chasing down her spine. But who wouldn't be thrilled at meeting him? she chided herself silently. For the past eight years Quinn Quartermain had been one of the most famous actors on screen and at thirty-seven had won countless awards for his work in the entertainment industry.

Ten years ago, he'd been just another struggling actor. Then his brilliant portrayal of Joshua Springfield in the blockbuster movie *Tales of Glory* had brought him to the attention of the world, and his talents had been in demand ever since.

During the past two years, he'd been directing, taking his genius behind the camera. Although audiences had missed seeing his strong, charismatic presence on the screen, his work to date had left the critics hard-pressed to find anything to criticize. Perhaps that was the reason they seemed willing to find fault now, April thought with a frown.

The sound of a car's tires crunching on the driveway outside brought her thoughts to a halt. A car door slammed and moments later Greg burst into the cabin.

'Hi.' April said, rising from the armchair.

'Hey, Sis. How's it going?' Greg asked as he discarded his jean jacket and headed for the kitchen.

'Fine. How was your evening?'

Greg was studying the contents of the refrigerator. 'Mark's folks have a VCR. We watched a great movie.'

'Want some tea?' April asked, filling the kettle and putting it on the stove.

'Sure,' came the muffled reply as Greg bit into a hunk of cheese. He grabbed an apple and let the door swing shut.

'What movie?' As she spoke, April removed two mugs from the cupboard.

'It was totally gruesome . . . about a guy who stalked these girls — '

'Enough,' April cut in. This time a cold shiver chased down her spine. She couldn't for the life of her understand what was appealing about being scared to death. She'd experienced that clawing fear firsthand, and had found nothing pleasant about it.

'Aw, come on, April, it was only a movie,' Greg said, sitting down at the kitchen table.

'I'd rather watch a good love story with Cary Grant and Ingrid Bergman or Jimmy Stewart and — '

'Who are they?' Greg flashed a quick grin at his sister's surprised stare.

'Brat!' she said, just as the kettle on the stove began to whistle.

'Are there any of Mom's scones left?' Greg asked as he finished off the apple.

'In the tin,' April said, pointing to the table. 'You know, Mom's right,' she added.

'About what?'

'You must have hollow legs. You devoured three-quarters of that pizza I bought for supper and I'll bet you ate at Mark's while you watched that disgusting movie. And here you are again

18

filling your face.'

'I'm a growing boy, that's all,' he told her as he proceeded to spread butter on three scones.

April smiled as she watched him. At fourteen, almost fifteen, Greg was fast losing his boyish appearance. Though he was small in stature, April was sure that before long he would surpass her height of five foot eight. He looked so much like their father that a wave of pain caught at her heart. Victor St. Clair had died of a heart attack four years before and there were still times, like now, that April found it hard to believe he was gone.

Greg had inherited his father's looks, from the kindly brown eyes and brown hair to the stubborn thrust of his chin. April, on the other hand, took after her grandmother, having the same classic features, enhanced by shoulder-length hair the color of rich dark chocolate, and eyes that some-times looked hazel and sometimes almost a moss green.

'So what did you do all evening?' Greg asked.

'Nothing much,' April answered as she poured tea into the two mugs. 'I was going to unpack, but Ian called.'

'What did he want?'

'A favor,' she replied, sitting down opposite Greg.

'Like what?'

'Like letting a friend of his come and stay with us for a while.'

'I hope you said no,' Greg said, pushing his chair back and rising.

'Why?' April asked, amused at her brother's reaction.

'Because . . . I don't know. Who is it, anyway?'

'Before I answer that, may I ask you something?'

'What?' Greg frowned.

'How good are you at keeping a secret?'

Greg scowled at his sister. 'The best,' he assured her. 'Anyway it isn't a secret anymore if you tell someone.'

'True,' she agreed, pleased with his

answer. 'What if I were to tell you that Quinn Quartermain was coming here — that he's the guest I've been talking about?'

'Quinn Quartermain! You mean *the* Quinn Quartermain?' Greg studied his sister for a long moment. 'Naw . . . you're pulling my leg. But wait a minute! Ian went to school with him, right? He was even at Ian's wedding . . . I remember Mom telling me that — which means you're not kidding.' He was smiling now, his eyes alight with excitement. 'Oh boy! Wait till I tell the guys — ' He stopped, his smile vanishing as suddenly as it came. 'You don't want me to tell anyone. Right?'

April nodded. 'He's still recovering from that accident, and the reason he's coming here is to get away from reporters and fans alike.'

'I suppose you can't blame him,' Greg commented. 'The press have been pretty hard on him. He hasn't given any interviews or anything. But heck, his girlfriend got killed — that's pretty heavy.'

'I agree,' April said, surprised and more than a little pleased at the compassionate note in her brother's voice.

'Someone's bound to spot him and ask who he is,' Greg said thoughtfully. 'I know! We can just say he's your boyfriend or fiancé or whatever David is — ' Greg stopped and studied his sister. 'Does David know about this?'

'How could he?' April asked.

'Are you going to tell him?' There was a gleam of interest in Greg's eyes.

April frowned. 'I don't know,' she answered truthfully. She'd forgotten about David. No, that wasn't strictly true, she amended; after all, they'd been engaged for the past six months. But David was a journalist for a Seattle newspaper, and therein lay the problem.

'I don't know.' She repeated the words softly, turning away from Greg to stand at the sink. David was first and foremost a reporter and an ambitious one at that, she reminded herself. She raked long fingers through her hair, stopping to massage the back of her neck in a gesture that told of her agitation. There was no reason to tell him, and every reason not to, she thought. Her hand grew still for a moment as the significance of this decision began to register.

'When is Quinn coming?' Greg's question cut into April's troubling thoughts, but it was several seconds before she answered.

'Well, Ian plans to drive. I'd say they should be here Sunday night, maybe Monday morning.'

'Wow! I can't believe it! Quinn Quartermain living in my house!' Greg's expression was one of wonder.

'That's if all goes well,' April said, trying to be practical. 'The press might catch on and prevent the whole thing. Even if he does make it here all right, after a few days of peace and quiet he may want to go back to L.A.' But April's cautionary words did little to dampen Greg's excitement.

'It's late. Hit the sheets, little brother,' April said, keeping her tone light.

Later, as April roamed the cabin turning out the lights, she stopped for a moment at the large picture window and stood staring out at the night. She found her thoughts turning to that first meeting with Quinn. Throughout the evening, the memory had slowly been wending its way to the surface of her mind; now it wanted free reign.

She and her mother had driven to Los Angeles to attend Ian and Jane's wedding. April had been asked to be one of the bridesmaids and she was beside herself with nervous anticipation at the thought of playing a role in the ceremony. Wedding dresses and weddings themselves had fascinated her for as long as she could remember.

Her bridesmaid's dress was a delicate shade of rose pink, its full skirt reaching to the floor and its lace bodice a dainty strapless creation.

At sixteen, the youngest of the

bridesmaids, April felt somewhat awkward, unsophisticated and more than a little awed by what was happening around her.

The ceremony itself was touchingly beautiful. April thought Ian and Jane made the most exquisite couple. Jane's dress, with its bodice of Victorian lace and its numerous petticoats, was breathtaking.

The reception, held at a well-known hotel in downtown L.A., seemed to April to be decidedly glamorous. The room was large, spacious and easily accommodated the two hundred guests. Each table was beautifully decorated with tiny vases of pink and white rosebuds and as she sat amid the wedding party at the head table, somehow April knew this would be a night she would never forget.

It had been later during the dancing that her mother remembered their wedding gift for Ian and Jane. Because they'd arrived late the night before, Laura St. Clair had locked the gift in the trunk of her car for safekeeping. However, amid the bustle and excitement of the day's proceedings, the package had slipped her mind.

April offered to go down to the hotel's underground parking garage and retrieve it. She'd left the ballroom and taken the elevator to the basement. The entire day had been one of the most wonderful of her life and April was feeling buoyant, as if she had been indulging in the champagne that had been served throughout the evening.

As she made her way toward the car, she heard whispered voices somewhere nearby. Her heart lurched and her steps slowed. She gripped the keys until they bit painfully into her palm, and as she drew nearer to her mother's tan Chevy, two figures suddenly appeared from the shadows.

April came to a standstill and her breath caught in her throat. The two dark-haired young men wore blue jeans and black sleeveless T-shirts, and April was instantly aware of the leering glances and knowing smiles as they moved toward her.

Her feet seemed glued to the ground as her fear created a trap of its own — immobility. She felt as if she were frozen in time, like an image on film when the shutter is pressed.

At that moment the sound of an approaching car broke through the stillness. As the lights from the vehicle swept over them, the two young men quickly turned and ran. April stood rooted to the spot.

Seconds later the driver stood before her, concern etched on his face.

'Are you all right?' he asked. The tone of his voice was soft and comforting and broke the paralyzing spell April had been under. She swayed, and he caught her, holding her gently but firmly against him. It was several long moments before April felt strong enough to stand on her own.

'I'm sorry,' she mumbled as she stepped out of his arms.

'Don't be sorry. You had quite a

scare,' her rescuer replied.

'If you hadn't come along . . . ' Her voice trailed off. She was unwilling to think about what might have happened, let alone put the thought into words.

'But I did come along,' he said and then smiled, an action which had a very strange effect on her heartbeat. It seemed to stop in midbeat, then trip over itself in an effort to regain its normal pace.

'How can I ever thank you?' April said, wishing she could stop trembling.

'By remembering never to allow yourself to become so vulnerable again.' He spoke the words evenly, his gaze holding hers, his message clear.

'I'll remember,' she vowed.

'Good!' Again he smiled and for a brief second April found herself wishing she was older and more sophisticated. The shock was beginning to wear off, and she was suddenly aware of the fact that her rescuer was a man in his late twenties.

The word 'attractive' didn't begin to

describe him. His eyes were the color of liquid gold, his hair a coppery shade of brown and his sharply defined features gave an impression of both strength and sensuality.

'What were you doing down here in the first place?' he asked.

'I came to get a wedding gift that was left in my mother's car,' she explained.

'Go and collect it while I park my car,' he told her. 'Then I'll walk with you to the elevator.'

April went over to the car and got the gift.

'Are the bride and groom Ian and Jane, by any chance?' her rescuer asked as he joined her once more.

'Why, yes,' April said. 'Do you know them?'

'Ian and I went to school together,' he explained. 'My name is Quinn Quartermain and you are . . . '

'April St. Clair,' she told him. 'Ian and I are cousins.'

The elevator door opened and April stepped in, followed by Quinn. During the short journey to the reception, Quinn asked April about the ceremony, smiling as she described the scene.

By the time they reached the door of the ballroom April felt relaxed, the tension from the encounter with the youths already fading from her mind. She thanked Quinn once again and watched as he made his way across the floor to Ian and Jane.

For the next hour April talked with relatives and danced with several young men, but all the while she was conscious of Quinn's presence in the room. She watched as he danced with Jane, then with the mothers of the bride and groom, and she found herself wishing he would ask her to dance. He was by far the most devastatingly handsome man she'd ever met.

When he appeared at her side sometime later, her heart began to flutter madly, like the wings of a baby bird before it makes its first flight. She smiled tentatively in greeting and let herself be drawn into his arms.

Throughout the entire dance she was only conscious of the man holding her, the way his lean body pressed lightly but firmly against hers, and the latent strength behind his gentle grasp.

During those moments in the basement when he'd held her, she'd been numb with shock. Here on the dance floor she was aware of him in an entirely different way. The woodsy fragrance of his cologne mingled with another tantalizing scent, making her feel strangely breathless. She only knew she wanted the music to go on forever. She wanted to stay in the circle of his arms and experience these new and wonderful sensations.

But the night ended all too quickly and it wasn't until the following day that April found out her rescuer was a struggling actor.

For April, this discovery added an aura of romanticism to Quinn. She found herself thinking of him as her knight in shining armor, and for a long time afterward freely admitted to herself that she had fallen a little in love with Quinn that night.

But she wasn't in love with him now. Ten years had passed — ten years in which she'd changed from an awkward and somewhat immature young girl into the woman she was today.

She'd had a crush on him, that was all, understandable because of the circumstances, but teenage crushes rarely developed into everlasting love.

Quinn's present circumstances aroused her compassion and by offering to help she was merely returning a kindness.

Besides, there was David. Abruptly her thoughts came to a halt and she turned from the window. Her fingers began to toy with the diamond and ruby ring on the fourth Finger of her left hand. When David had proposed to her six months ago she'd accepted. But during these past months when she'd been pushing herself to the limit, when she'd needed his support, his love and understanding, he'd only become more demanding, stepping up his campaign to break down the physical barriers she'd imposed on their relationship. She wanted to wait, to save herself for their wedding night and by so doing give him the greatest gift a woman could offer the man she loved — total love and trust.

Was she being naive in expecting him to understand? She had asked herself this question numerous times, but had found no answer.

Surely David could understand that her career and the success of her boutique were as important to her as his own career was to him! She'd told him that the Santini wedding would be both challenging and demanding and would take up a good portion of her and Bobbi's time. But right from the outset she had known he'd resented having to play second fiddle to her work. When she'd jokingly pointed out to him the numerous times he'd broken a date with her in order to go on an assignment, he hadn't been in the least amused. She shook her head at the memory.

She'd thought that being in love, truly in love, the everlasting kind of love she'd always dreamed existed, would be a love without doubts, without questions — unconditional.

Now, suddenly, all she had were doubts and unanswered questions. What did it mean?

2

'It's too bad he quit acting,' Greg said as he joined April in the kitchen late the next morning.

'Who?' April asked, though she knew full well whom Greg was talking about.

'Quinn Quartermain, of course,' came the reply as Greg poured cereal into a bowl and added milk. 'He was the best. Did you see that spy movie he was in . . . ? What was it called?'

'*Deception Runs Deep*,' April responded, obligingly providing the title. It had been the last movie Quinn had appeared in and, as with all his movies, she had seen it not once but several times.

'That's it! He played a CIA agent who uncovered a plot to kill the president. But when he took the evidence to his superiors they immediately locked him away because the head of intelligence was in on the assassination plot. It was great. Boy, imagine, Quinn Quartermain here! I sure wish I could tell the guys.' Greg sighed.

'I know how you feel, Greg, but the minute you tell someone it's sure to get around the neighborhood and eventually leak to the press.'

'Yeah, I guess so,' he conceded.

'Just try to forget about it for now,' she suggested. 'What's on the agenda for today?' she asked, changing the subject.

'There's a high school football game this afternoon,' he answered.

'Hey, didn't you try out for the team?' April asked as she poured cream into her coffee.

'I tried out,' came the gruff reply. 'But I didn't make it.' He roughly pushed back his chair and stood up.

'Greg! I'm sorry. I didn't know,' April said sympathetically.

'It doesn't matter,' Greg muttered, noisily dropping the bowl and spoon into the sink. 'I didn't want to play on the crummy football team anyway.'

Yes, you did, April thought, seeing the hurt on his face. She wished for a moment she could pull him into her arms and comfort him, as she had done on numerous occasions when he'd been younger. But to do that would only increase his annoyance and undoubtedly embarrass him. Thoughtfully April sipped her coffee.

'That's a tough break, Greg,' she commiserated. 'Still, there's always next year. Besides, I've never been able to understand why a bunch of supposedly intelligent young men would want to chase a ball in the first place.'

Her comment brought a ghost of a smile to his features. 'I guess I'll go along and watch,' Greg said. 'Mark made the team,' he added, and April found herself wondering if that, too, was not a thorn in his side. 'Anyway, there's really not much else to do around here on a Saturday.'

'I could find you something to do,' April offered. 'How about cleaning out the garage, or tidying up your room, or — '

'Sorry, Sis, got to go.' Greg grinned as he pulled on his jean jacket. 'Jason phoned when you were in the shower. His dad's going to drop us off at the game on his way to Bellingham.'

'That's good. When can I expect to see you? Supper time?'

'Maybe, maybe not.' Greg hesitated in the open doorway.

'Greg,' April cautioned. 'Just let me know where you'll be later and if you need a ride home I'll come and get you.'

'Yes, Mother,' Greg replied sweetly, then dodged the dish towel April threw at him.

April began tidying up after Greg left. The cabin was large and roomy. Of log construction, it appeared rustic and was quite simply quaint. The old stone fireplace in the living room was blackened with use and the furnishings, though not elaborate, had warmth and character.

April turned her attention to the guest room. As she put fresh linen on the bed and hung clean towels in the adjoining bathroom, she found herself wondering if perhaps Quinn would find these living quarters a trifle too rustic. No doubt he was used to more luxurious surroundings.

At two o'clock April was hungry and called a halt to her efforts. She'd long since finished tidying the cabin and for the past hour had been working in the garage in an attempt to make space for her own car next to her mother's vehicle. During the winter months, the damp air, and especially the fog that often rolled in from the ocean played havoc with the paint on a car. Putting it in the garage offered some measure of protection.

Back in the kitchen she grilled a cheese sandwich and poured herself a tall glass of milk. She had just bitten into the sandwich when the telephone rang.

April stared at it for a moment.

Swallowing quickly, she reached for the receiver.

'Hello.'

'Hi, darling.'

'David? Hi!'

'Don't sound so surprised,' David said, a faint hint of annoyance in his tone, 'especially when I called to apologize.'

'Apologize? For what?' April asked.

'For being so abrupt with you yesterday when you called, of course,' he explained. 'I was in a rotten mood and I took it out on you. I'm sorry, darling.'

'That's all right. We all have our moments. But why were you in a bad mood?' she asked.

'I'd been trying to get through to Billy Cotton, a reporter friend of mine in L.A. He's been covering the story of Sasha Gray's death and I wanted to find out whether or not Quartermain was agreeing to any interviews yet.' At David's words April dropped into the chair nearby and her heart began to pound in her ears.

'And?' April asked cautiously.

'No dice,' came the abrupt reply. 'Boy, I can't help wondering if there isn't something fishy about that accident. My guess is he was drinking. I was planning to fly down there, but there's not much point. Billy said Quartermain was released from the hospital yesterday and he's still refusing to make a statement. What I'd give for a chance to talk to him!'

At David's words her heart sank. She hadn't considered that he might be assigned to cover this particular story. David's attitude, too, reflected that of the stories she'd already read about Quinn, and suddenly, unaccountably, April felt a sense of protectiveness for Quinn.

'But the police say it was an accident,' April stated, coming to Quinn's defense.

'I didn't call to talk about my work, darling,' David said. 'I called to see if you arrived safe and sound.'

41

'Yes, thank you, I did,' April replied, annoyed at the way he brushed her comment aside.

'I still don't understand why Greg couldn't have stayed with a friend while your mother is away,' she heard David say.

'We've been through this before, David. I promised Mother I'd be here. There's nothing more to say.' April fought to keep the exasperation from her voice.

'I know. It's just that my parents want us to spend Thanksgiving with them,' David added.

'Then the solution is to invite Greg, too,' April answered, annoyance flickering through her once again.

'Don't be silly, darling.' David laughed. 'A fourteen-year-old kid who spends his time listening to loud rock music and who has little regard for other people's property would not be my mother's idea of an ideal guest at Thanksgiving dinner.'

'He's my brother, David,' April

reminded him, shocked by his attitude. Though she knew Greg and David had not exactly hit it off when she'd brought David to Birch Bay during the summer, she was surprised to discover that his resentment over an incident that had happened then still lingered.

At the time April remembered thinking that David had overreacted. From the moment they arrived, Greg had openly admired David's camera equipment. Eager to show the camera to his friends who'd come to collect him for an outing to the water slides nearby, Greg had removed it from its case. He should have asked permission, of course, because the camera was an expensive one, but nothing untoward had happened. David, however, had angrily chastised Greg in front of his friends — an action that had instantly alienated the boy. For the remainder of their visit, Greg practically ignored David to the point of rudeness. But the fact that David still bore a grudge troubled her a great deal.

'Don't sound so disapproving, darling,' David's lightly scolding tone cut into April's thoughts. 'When Greg joins the human race I'm sure we'll get along splendidly. Anyway, we're practically family now. You just have to set the date.'

April bit back a sigh. 'You promised you wouldn't pressure me.'

'And I'm not. I'm being very patient,' David replied, sounding hurt. 'I'd better go. I'll give you a call in a day or so. Take care. Bye.'

April replaced the receiver, a jumble of emotions running through her, making it difficult to pinpoint exactly what she was feeling. Take care — the words echoed in her head. What about I love you? she thought.

David had said it only once so far, on the night he'd proposed. Shouldn't people who are in love say those words to each other often? Damn! What was the matter with her? She loved him, didn't she? Didn't she? She held her breath, waiting for an answer. She'd been asking herself that question a lot lately. Perhaps being away from him would help her put their relationship into perspective. Perhaps . . .

Abruptly April rose from the chair, willing her troubled thoughts away. Her appetite gone, she tossed the barely eaten sandwich into the garbage. She opened the refrigerator to return the carton of milk, then stood for a moment studying the contents. Though her mother had said she'd shopped several days ago the shelves looked sadly depleted.

She thought of the food she'd seen Greg put away and smiled. Shopping was a must, she decided, especially when Ian and Quinn might well arrive at supper time on Sunday.

Glad to have something to occupy her time, April quickly compiled a list and was soon on her way to the grocery store in the border town of Blaine.

★ ★ ★

Quinn stuffed the half-eaten hamburger back into the paper bag. He wasn't hungry. It was already late Saturday afternoon and they had been on the road since before dawn, stopping only to grab a bite and then only at drive-through restaurants.

Quinn hadn't slept, and he couldn't remember a time when he felt more tired. His exhaustion was not from exertion but from denying himself the sleep his body craved. Each time he closed his eyes a picture of Sasha appeared before him, and inside his head echoed the sound of her voice screaming his name.

Quinn had readily agreed to Ian's idea to smuggle him from the house and no doubt because of its simplicity, the plan had succeeded.

Under cover of darkness Ian had quietly opened the rear door of his car. Keeping low, Quinn had crossed the short distance from the front door to the car, climbed in and crouched on the floor. After throwing a car blanket over

Quinn, Ian had closed the door. Walking around to the driver's side he'd climbed in and, after a perfunctory wave to Robson, had driven off.

As the car began to gather speed, Quinn had suddenly felt his skin grow cold and the sour taste of bile fill his mouth. Perspiration broke out all over his body as his mind struggled in a vain attempt to remember something. But what? The memory danced on the outer edges of his mind, tantalizingly near. The clamminess that washed over him told him fear was the emotion he was experiencing. But fear of what? The memory floated out of reach once more and for a moment, Quinn had thought he might pass out.

The sound of Ian's voice triumphantly telling him they had made it through the reporters without a hitch brought him back to reality. Awkwardly Quinn removed the blanket covering him and rose gingerly from the floor of the car. He had to take several deep, steadying breaths before his heart rate returned to normal and the nausea finally receded.

That had been last night. Each time he thought of those stifling moments in the back of the car, a faint flicker of a memory caused a shudder to pass through his frame. He'd tried to force his mind to remember — succeeding only in intensifying the pain that was throbbing through his head. But for the first time since waking in the hospital, he began to believe that his memory would return and that one day the secret of those missing hours would be revealed.

Glancing now at Ian, he knew that his friend must be tired, but the desire to put as much distance between himself and Los Angeles prevented him from suggesting that they stop to rest. Another reason, far less tangible than the first, and which bordered on paranoia, was the sense that they were being followed.

Quinn made no mention of this to Ian, but as the hours passed and miles were eaten up, he couldn't for the life of him shake the unsettling feeling. Perhaps he'd been in too many movies — or perhaps, as a result of the accident, his instincts were ultrasensitive — but something deep inside told him he was right.

It was late evening when they reached Portland and Ian suggested they stop for the night. As Ian pulled into the driveway of a second-rate motel, Quinn twisted in his seat, trying to survey the street behind them in the hope of catching sight of something, anything that would confirm his suspicions. It was dark and the drizzle of moisture that had started to fall over an hour before was now a steady rain, making it nearly impossible to distinguish one car from another.

Quinn watched the dark shape of a vehicle as it appeared to slow down, edging its way past the motel driveway. His heart started to pound and he reached for the door handle, forgetting for the moment that his arm was in a cast. Pain, sharp and agonizing, ripped through him.

'What happened? Are you all right?' Ian asked, staring anxiously at his friend.

Quinn cradled his arm, waiting for the pain to recede. 'Yes . . . yes,' he repeated. 'I just moved a little too quickly.'

'Wait here, I'll register,' Ian said as he eased himself from the car.

Quinn slowly turned to study the street once more, but the traffic was moving normally and there was no sign of the vehicle.

Long after Ian had fallen asleep, Quinn lay staring at the television set watching a rerun of an old detective series. His body desperately cried out for sleep but Sasha's image continued to haunt him.

What a future she'd have had. What incredible talent! Lost now, forever. Why?

His head was beginning to feel as if someone was pounding it with sledge-hammers, and he slid from the bed to pour himself another ounce of Scotch from the bottle Ian had thoughtfully provided.

Leaning back against the pillows once more, he tried to concentrate on the low murmur of voices coming from the television screen, but his mind refused to comply and he found his thoughts turning in a different direction.

April . . . His lips moved in a fragment of a smile. Strange that he would meet her again. He could still recall the moment when he had first seen her, looking like a frightened young doe that was trapped in the beam of his headlights, waiting for the lion — or lions in this case — to pounce. The two youths had quickly made their escape, and much as he had wanted to chase them, their potential victim had needed him more.

She had nearly fainted, which was understandable in the circumstances, and as he held her, waiting for the fear to subside, he remembered thinking how fragile she felt in his arms. She'd been sixteen, seventeen perhaps, a girl poised on the edge of womanhood, the promise of loveliness gradually making itself known.

Funny that he could remember everything about that long-gone evening, while the events of the evening less than a week ago were shrouded in mystery.

Stop it! he berated himself. Time was a great healer — wasn't that what they said? He prayed silently that it was true. For the next few days at least, his mind and body would be granted the chance to begin healing.

His memory had to return — there were no ifs, ands or buts about it. One way or another he had to know if he could have avoided the collision . . . if there was something he could have done . . .

The throbbing pain in his temples was steadily building to a crescendo. Gulping down the remainder of the Scotch, he eased himself from the bed and this time carried the bottle back with him. Perhaps if he drank enough he would, temporarily at least, escape from the pain, the frustration and the horrible guilt. Surely anything would be better than the hell he was living now.

3

April had never known a day go by so slowly in her life. Nervous anticipation manifested itself in its usual way, so she spent the best part of Sunday in the kitchen preparing a beef stew, stuffed baked potatoes, and pineapple upside-down cake, not to mention another batch of scones to replace the ones Greg had devoured. April had doubled her usual recipe for the stew, but as she cleared away the pots she had to shake her head when she saw how little there was left. Growing boy, indeed!

Greg, too, had been restless all day. He had hung around the cabin, continually watching the road for the arrival of a car with California license plates.

At eight-thirty, Greg, who had been finishing his homework in the kitchen, closed his books, then grabbed an apple from the refrigerator before settling down to watch television.

April turned her attention back to the fashion magazines in her lap and tried hard to concentrate on the sketch pad she was holding. But for the first time in her life, the challenge of a new creation did not captivate her.

At ten-thirty, April finally had to shoo Greg off to bed.

'Maybe they're not coming tonight,' Greg said, standing in the bathroom doorway brushing his teeth.

'It's beginning to look that way,' April agreed.

Greg's figure retreated into the bathroom, then emerged a few moments later. 'They could have had a flat tire or something. Maybe you should drive toward the freeway . . . '

'Greg! I am not driving anywhere.' April exclaimed in an exasperated tone. 'Even if I did, I don't remember what Ian's car looks like. They'll get here. Now, go to bed. You have school tomorrow.' Distractedly, she drew her hand through her hair.

'Okay! Okay! I just wanted to see him, that's all.' Greg slouched off to his room, leaving April feeling guilty that she had snapped at him. Her own short temper was a result of a day spent on tenterhooks, and she freely admitted to herself that she was just as anxious as Greg to have their guest arrive.

With Greg in bed, April returned to the living room and switched channels on the television to the evening news. She attempted to pay attention to the newscaster, but the voice on the screen droned on and soon April was no longer listening.

She wasn't sure how long she had been sitting there half dozing, but the sound of a car pulling into the driveway alerted her instantly.

She sat listening for a moment, then stood up and moved to the door. Outside the air was decidedly cold and the silence that met her as she opened the door made her hesitate. *Had* she heard a car? The drumming rhythm she could hear, she suddenly realized, was the sound of her own heart beating frantically.

Rounding the corner of the house, she came to a halt as she saw a car parked alongside the garage. The engine was silent and the interior was in darkness. Frowning, April wished she had thought to grab the flashlight her mother kept by the door.

Hesitating to move forward, she stood waiting, watching as the car door opened and a dark, shadowy figure slowly, awkwardly climbed out.

He was wearing a bulky wool sweater over a pair of jeans, but in the faint light from the car's interior April could not identify the man. His clothing blended into the darkness, and only when he turned toward her did the first glimmer of recognition begin to stir. Her pulse skipped crazily for a second as his profile came into view.

When his eyes met hers she knew instantly it was Quinn. 'Golden fire' was how they had once been described and April remembered thinking just how apt a description it was. But tonight Quinn's eyes lacked the golden glow his many fans found so appealing. Tonight his eyes looked . . . haunted — that was the word that leaped to mind, for he looked pale and gaunt and very tired.

Something about him looked different, April thought as she continued her study. He seemed taller than she remembered, and his hair was longer, curling over the edges of his sweater. Then she noticed the beginnings of a mustache and beard darkening the lower portion of his face.

As Quinn carefully stepped from the car, he drew a deep breath. The cold night air temporarily chased away the feeling of exhaustion that had come over him during the last few miles of his journey. There had been moments when he thought he'd never make it, when he'd caught himself dropping off to sleep. But he'd forced himself to watch for the landmarks Ian had mentioned, the seven or eight sets of stop signs, the small bridge, and lastly the white fence surrounding the cabin.

It was several seconds before he noticed the figure standing nearby, watching him. He froze in his tracks. It was a woman, that much he knew, but he couldn't quite define her features, only the silhouette of her hair framing her face.

'Are you all right?' April moved closer, concern evident in her tone.

Quinn shook his head as if to clear it. The voice was soft and soothing. 'I'm just tired,' he replied.

'Where's Ian?' April asked. 'I thought he was coming with you?'

'He did,' Quinn replied, then, holding his injured arm against his body, he moved past April to the trunk of the car.

'I'll do that,' April offered, noticing now the white plaster protruding below the sleeve of the sweater.

Quinn reluctantly relinquished the keys and moved aside. 'Ian drove most of the way,' he explained. 'We stopped at Bellingham Airport about eight to check on the flight times to L.A. They told him there was one leaving at nine. I managed to persuade him to take it.' Quinn's tone was edged with weariness, as if persuading Ian had perhaps been a difficult task.

'I see,' April said. Lifting the suitcase from the trunk, she wondered why it had taken Quinn over two hours to drive to the cabin; the trip from the airport could usually be done in less than one.

'This way,' April murmured and, suitcase in hand, she walked along the side of the cabin.

April held the door for Quinn then closed it quietly behind him. 'Can I offer you something to eat or drink?' she asked, setting the suitcase on the floor.

'I think I'll pass,' Quinn said, turning to face her. 'The drive was tiring.'

April was instantly apologetic. 'Of course, forgive me,' she said. 'The guest room is this way.' She grasped the suitcase once more and moved down the hall. Under the brighter lights of the cabin, April had seen the fatigue etched on his face and noted the pain in his eyes. The fresh growth of beard, which appeared to be rust colored, while serving to emphasize his rather bedraggled appearance, added a new dimension to the strong character of his face. Setting his suitcase on the chest at the foot of the bed, April turned and smiled. 'I hope you'll be comfortable,' she said.

'Thank you, April.' He glanced around the room. 'I'm afraid my manners have been somewhat lacking. Forgive me,' he said softly.

'That's all right.' April was warmed by his words. 'I'd just like to say how sorry — '

'Thank you,' Quinn's voice cut in.

She saw the despair in his eyes and the cold, shuttered expression on his face. The message was all too clear. He wanted to be alone. But instead of feeling rebuffed, April felt a strong urge to reach out and touch him, to hold him gently in his arms, as he had done for her so long ago.

Their eyes met and held for several seconds, causing April's heart to skip a beat. 'I'll wish you good night, then,' she said and moved toward the door.

'April.' Quinn spoke her name softly. It seemed to roll off his tongue. She'd become a beautiful woman, he thought as he watched her turn to face him. 'I really don't know how to thank you.'

She smiled at him. Suddenly Quinn wished he was able to capture the image of purity her smile seemed to hold. 'Glad to help,' he heard her say before the door closed, leaving him staring after her.

The unmistakable sincerity in her voice somehow seemed to soothe him and he smiled to himself as he turned to survey the room. It was plainly furnished, a double bed, a chest of drawers, the old trunk where April had placed his suitcase, and yet there was a warmth and homeyness about the room that brought a sigh of contentment to his lips. He liked its rustic quality, its lack of pretension, and he liked the feeling of openness afforded by the set of sliding glass doors that looked out onto the rocky beachfront.

He unlocked the door, which slid back easily, and stood staring at the ocean, which looked black and was almost invisible but for silvery glints of light that danced across its glassy surface.

The air felt cool and fresh against his face, and whimsically Quinn found himself wishing he would never have to go back. He turned into the room, closing the door and the curtains, shutting out the night, but not the thoughts that were beginning to crowd into his head once more.

God, but he was tired. The drive from the airport had been grueling, and Ian had taken some convincing that the best course of action was for him to return to Los Angeles and for

Quinn to go on alone.

Quinn wasn't sure he'd ever be able to tell Ian how much their friendship meant to him. They had met in high school when they'd both tried out for the football team. Neither had made it, but had soon become fast friends. Their friendship had weathered the test of time and remained constant throughout Quinn's highly publicized career. He had no family of his own — not since the death of his father nearly seven years before. Over the years, Ian, Jane and the boys had become his family. Quinn visited them as often as his busy schedule permitted. Recently, though, Quinn had found himself envying Ian and his family life, when the loneliness he felt became too much to bear.

During the hour before his plane departed, Ian had carefully outlined the route Quinn should travel in order to find Birch Bay and the small resort owned and operated by Laura St. Clair. No one seemed to pay particular attention to either of them as they sat in a quiet corner of the coffee shop, and Quinn found himself wondering if perhaps he had simply been overreacting when he'd thought they were being followed.

Just the same, he was a man who lived by his instincts and he was unwilling to ignore them now. After seeing Ian off, Quinn returned to the car. For nearly an hour he sat in the darkness, watching the somewhat sporadic flow of travellers arriving and departing.

Cold, stiff and aching he started the engine, then had to sit for several minutes while the heater's warmth gradually restored mobility to his limbs. He drove south, back into Bellingham until he found a drive-in restaurant where he placed his order. He barely touched the food — junk food, never a favorite with him, had lost what little appeal it had.

Back on the freeway, he headed north and had no trouble following Ian's instructions. Then, during the last five miles, after leaving the freeway, another car's headlights suddenly appeared in his rearview mirror.

It was absurd, of course. The car hadn't been following him. It was all in his imagination — and undoubtedly contributing to his state of mind had been the fact that the last movie he'd directed had been a murder mystery.

As he got ready for bed, Quinn rubbed his chin and for a brief moment was surprised to feel the rough texture of his beard. Growing the beard had not been a conscious choice but one that evolved out of pure necessity. Bathing and shaving, rituals any man took for granted, had for him become practically impossible. Though trying to keep the plaster cast on his arm dry was a fine art, it was not impossible. Shaving *was* impossible! And anyway, he rationalized, a beard would help hide his identity.

Not without difficulty, Quinn removed his clothes and crawled between the sheets. He lay on his back, resting his arm on one of the pillows; for the first time in days the throbbing in his head had diminished to a dull ache.

There had been no miracle. His memory had not returned. Since departing from L.A., he'd found himself harboring the notion that the moment he arrived in Birch Bay his memory would miraculously return and he would be free from this torment of not knowing, of not remembering. But now he saw his hope was only a foolish dream. His lips curled in a bitter smile.

There was one consolation, though. For the first time since waking up in hospital Quinn felt in control of his life. His memory *would* return. He had to believe it!

His eyelids began to droop, his breathing deepened and as he sank into the realms of sleep, the sleep his body cried out for, an image of April's smile danced across his mind — and in the darkness his expression relaxed.

4

'Are they here?' Greg asked in hushed tones as he joined April in the kitchen the next morning. 'There's a car outside. They must be here,' he added, answering his own question.

'Yes and no,' April said, trying not to smile at the puzzled expression on her brother's face.

'What do you mean?'

'Quinn is here, but Ian is already back in L.A.,' April explained.

'Quinn's here?' Greg ignored the latter part of April's statement. 'When did he arrive? Was it very late? What's he like?' Greg fired the questions at her.

April popped two slices of bread into the toaster and turned to him. 'Which question would you like me to answer first?' she inquired, unable to resist teasing him.

'Come on, April. It isn't every day a

famous movie star comes to live with you, you know.'

April smiled. 'All right, let me see. It must have been about eleven-thirty. I'd dozed off on the sofa watching the news — '

'Never mind the news,' Greg cut in impatiently. 'How does he look?'

'Exhausted and in pain,' April said. And the pain is not all due to his injuries, she thought to herself, remembering the look of despair she'd seen in his eyes.

'And . . . ' Greg prompted, interrupting her thoughts.

'Well, he looks different. He's growing a beard.'

'Wow! A disguise,' Greg said instantly.

April laughed. 'I hadn't thought of that,' she said. 'It certainly changes his appearance, but I wouldn't be surprised if it's simply because he isn't able to shave. He did break his arm.'

'Oh! Right,' Greg said. 'But does he still look like he did in his movies?'

Frowning thoughtfully, April reached

for her coffee cup on the table. During the moments she'd been with Quinn, she had simply been aware of him as a man in need of help, in need of comfort . . . perhaps even in need of love.

'Hey! I'd say he bowled you over, Sis.' Greg laughed. 'Maybe I should give David a call and tell him you've fallen madly in love with a movie star.'

'Don't you dare!' The words sprang from April's lips and she glared at her brother.

'Wouldn't that be something?' Greg was lost in his own fantasy. 'Can you see me introducing Quinn to my friends?' He cleared his throat. 'Guys . . . I'd like you to meet my future brother-in-law, Quinn Quartermain.' Greg grinned. 'Boy, can't you just see their faces?'

April stood shaking her head at him.

'I was *only* kidding,' Greg said with a sigh, moving to grab the bread as it popped from the toaster. There was silence while Greg busied himself spreading peanut butter on his toast.

Then, looking at April, he ventured to ask, 'Do you think he's awake? I could take him a cup of coffee and introduce myself. What do you think?'

'I'm not sure that's a good idea,' April said gently, and seeing Greg's crestfallen expression she added: 'My bet is he'll sleep most of the morning. He certainly looked tired enough.'

'Will I see him tonight?' Disappointment was evident in the teenager's tone.

'I imagine so. This cabin isn't that big, you know.' April smiled at her brother. 'Don't forget, he's been through a great deal lately,' she said, her tone serious. 'We both know what it's like to lose someone you care for. He's come a long way for some peace and quiet. Let's give him the breathing space he needs.'

'You're right. It's just . . . '

'I know,' April replied. 'Not every fourteen-year-old gets to meet his movie idol — just the lucky ones.' She reached out to ruffle his hair.

'Hey! Don't do that. And I'm nearly fifteen,' he reminded her as he moved out of reach. 'I guess I'll get ready for school.' Turning, he sauntered off to his room.

After Greg left to catch the bus, April cleared up the breakfast dishes, then headed for the shower. Standing under the warm spray, she found herself thinking about her brother's reaction to Quinn's presence. Hero worship was certainly typical of a youth of Greg's age, but she hoped that while he was with his friends he would remember his promise to keep Quinn's identity a secret.

She wasn't entirely sure why she should harbor these strong protective instincts for a man she hardly knew. Her hands grew still and the soap slipped from her fingers. No! That wasn't strictly true.

Over the years she'd followed Quinn's career with great interest, watching his talent grow and develop, seeing the star emerge and admiring the strength of character that was so evident in the man himself. She'd never forgotten the thoughtful and caring way he had treated her on that night so long ago. Now was her chance to repay him, and she knew she would do everything in her power to give him the privacy and solitude he was seeking.

He must have loved Sasha Gray very much, she acknowledged, recalling the pain and despair she'd seen in his eyes. At this thought, she suddenly shivered and had to adjust the spray on the shower until warmth was restored.

Several minutes later, April emerged from the bathroom, her face free of makeup and her hair falling softly to her shoulders. She was dressed in a pair of faded blue jeans and a sweatshirt.

During the morning April began work on the sketches she'd had trouble with the evening before. The designs were for a wedding that would take place on Saint Valentine's Day. The prospective bride had definite ideas about what she wanted, and April was attempting to capture those ideas on paper. Outside the weather was windy and cold, the waters of the bay tossing up whitecaps. April found her attention constantly wandering from the task in hand.

At noon she warmed the beef stew she'd made the previous day. As she ate she found herself straining to hear a sound that would tell her Quinn was awake. Was he all right? she wondered.

This question prompted her to walk down the hall and stand outside his door, listening for the sound of movement from within. The sudden scream of a gull made her gasp in surprise, and as she withdrew she silently chastised herself for her foolishness. The man was exhausted and obviously needed to sleep.

Pulling on her ski jacket, she slipped from the cabin and made her way along the beach. A walk would help pass the time and perhaps clear some of the cobwebs from her mind. She'd always loved this time of year when the elements seemed to rise up in anger and subject the earth, together with its humble creatures, to various forms of punishment. It wasn't punishment at all, of course; the rain was necessary for the rejuvenation of the soil, as was the snow. And the wind acted as a gigantic broom sweeping the earth's surface, cleaning house, making ready for the new growth of spring.

April strode out across the rocky beach, the wind tugging playfully at her hair and sending it flying around her face. She had no particular destination in mind. She was simply heading toward Birch Bay State Park, which catered each summer to campers eager to explore this part of the Washington coastline.

As she passed the cabins spaced out along the beach, everything was decidedly peaceful and quiet, a far cry from the noise and bustle of the summer months.

The small resort her mother ran was made up of a dozen cabins, which were occupied on a week-to-week basis from mid-May to the end of September. For as long as April could remember, her parents had worked through the hot summer months, rarely taking a holiday of their own. The resort was their livelihood and for her mother it still was.

A gull gliding on the wind, suspended majestically in the air, captured April's attention and for a moment she marveled at the sight.

The wind was making her skin tingle and the restless feeling that had come over her seemed to have dissipated for the moment. It felt so good, so right to be home she thought, glancing at the white flashes of the waves as they broke the silvery gray of the water. She followed the path of a small motorboat that was making its way across the bay, and drawing a deep breath, she suddenly felt peaceful.

She'd been under a good deal of pressure lately, what with wanting to finish the dresses for the Santini wedding ahead of schedule so that she could come home. But it was more than that. She knew and understood the pressures connected with her work at the boutique, and even considered them a major part of the exciting challenge her work offered.

No — the unsettled, unhappy feelings she'd been having lately had nothing to do with work — but everything to do with David.

Thrusting her hands into her pockets she kicked at a rock at her feet. Lately it seemed that each time her thoughts turned to David, she felt herself grow tense, and a knot of anxiety would tighten inside her. A sigh broke from her lips and she felt the sting of tears behind her eyes. She blinked them away, wondering why she should suddenly feel sad and a little lost.

She'd met David a year ago at a gala bridal fair sponsored by a large hotel chain in Seattle. The fair was an annual event that attracted people from as far north as Vancouver, across the

Canadian border, to San Francisco in the south. She and Bobbi had worked frantically for several months, designing and sewing four wedding gowns for the fair.

The show had proven to be a great triumph for them. Their designs had been described as strikingly individual, exquisitely feminine and highly original.

David had been assigned to cover the fair and when he'd approached her to say he wanted to use the photographs he had taken of the designs, both she and Bobbi had been ecstatic. Ultimately the business the entire venture generated had helped to establish the boutique.

April had been grateful for the exposure David's article afforded, and when he called to ask if he might take her to dinner she had readily accepted. She found him a charming and attentive companion, and gradually they had slipped into a relationship that April found very comfortable.

She'd felt a kinship with him. Like

her, he was deeply involved with his career and therefore understood her commitment to the boutique.

When he asked her to marry him, she'd accepted. But the euphoria hadn't lasted. It seemed that since their engagement David had become both possessive of her time and more demanding of her attention.

What also troubled her was the fact that he'd begun to press her to give up what he considered to be her old-fashioned ideas about the physical side of their relationship. Most engaged couples slept together, he told her, and he saw no reason why they should wait. April had never slept with a man and she was proud of that fact, proud in the knowledge that she was keeping sacred the ultimate gift of love a woman could give the man she loved, the man she married.

She'd found it difficult to analyze her feelings as she listened to David's lighthearted, matter-of-fact tone. Some emotion must have registered on her face, for he had quickly taken her into his arms and assured her he had no intention of rushing her. But the words had been spoken, and April found herself confused and unaccountably let down. Perhaps that was why she had thrown herself wholeheartedly into the Santini project, filling the hours with work and spending less time with David.

When she'd explained to him about her mother's trip he'd received the news with barely concealed anger, and while she agreed that she probably should have consulted him, what she'd found distressing was David's unwillingness to see her point of view, or to compromise.

Dragging her hand through her windswept hair she tried, not for the first time, to put her feelings into perspective. Every relationship had its ups and downs; they were going through a rough patch, that was all. But as she gazed out over the water she found herself wondering more and more whether or not she really loved him. Surely, if that were the case the thought of making love with him should fill her with excitement, not trepidation!

Annoyed with herself, she bent to pick up a rock, then tossed it into the water. What was she afraid of? Picking up a handful of rocks, she threw them one by one into the ocean.

With a sigh she turned and headed back the way she had come. As she walked she noticed a truck pull into the driveway and stop. Who was her visitor? she wondered. Probably one of the neighbors, she thought, picking up her pace. She watched as the driver climbed from the cab and moved to peer into the car parked by the garage — Ian's car — the one Quinn had arrived in the previous night.

A cold shiver of alarm swept through her when she saw the stranger open the car door. 'Hey!' she yelled, breaking into a run. The man looked up, then slammed the car door, quickly returning to his truck and backing out of the driveway. Though April was closing the gap between them, she was still too far away to be able to see him clearly. By the time she reached the cabin, the truck was nowhere in sight.

Heart pounding, her breathing labored, she stood for a moment staring at the empty street, her mind a jumble of questions. Who had it been? A reporter? Surely not. But why was the man so interested in the car? Had he planned to steal it? Impossible! How could he drive two vehicles at once? But the question remained . . . Who was he?

Her thoughts in a turmoil, April entered the cabin and glanced at the clock above the fireplace. It was nearly two-thirty. Should she wake Quinn and tell him about the stranger? Shrugging out of her jacket she made her way down the hall.

* * *

Quinn turned on the water and stepped into the shower. He had awakened half an hour ago, and for the first time in what seemed an eternity the throbbing pain in his head was gone. He had slept, peacefully, dreamlessly, and his body felt rested, renewed.

He'd allowed himself the luxury of lying in bed, listening to the sound of the waves breaking on the shore and the occasional cry of a seabird.

Standing under the warm soothing spray, he turned his thoughts back to the night of the accident, taking his mind a step at a time through the events of that evening.

He and Sasha had flown back to L.A. together and after picking up his car, he had driven them both directly to the television studios, where they'd been scheduled to appear as guests on a late-night talk show.

When the show was over, he'd planned to slip away unnoticed, drive home and sleep for a week. He'd thought Sasha would stay for the party after the show, and had been surprised when she'd asked if he'd give her a lift to her apartment. It had been well past midnight when they made their way across the near-deserted parking lot.

He remembered unlocking the passenger door of his Mercedes but as always, it was at this juncture that his memory became decidedly hazy. His breath was coming in short gasps now and the ache in his head was once more a pounding reality. Taking deep, ragged breaths, he managed to pull himself back from the edge of the black void his memory had reached. He stood for several minutes, letting the water soothe his trembling body and calm his turbulent thoughts. But the exercise had not been totally fruitless. For a fleeting moment during those seconds of straining to catch a glimpse of the past, the blackness had suddenly evaporated to reveal a floating gray mist. He considered this a breakthrough; he refused to believe otherwise.

Holding his right arm aloft and out of harm's way he clumsily completed his shower, and when he turned off the water he was pleased to note that the pain in his head had grown more tolerable. Stepping onto the mat he grabbed the large bath towel with his left hand and dried his face. Accustomed now to the feel of his beard and mustache, he was glad not to have to shave. He towel-dried his hair, then awkwardly wrapped the towel around his waist.

Returning to the bedroom, he crossed to his suitcase and with his left hand began to fumble with the tiny tumblers of the combination lock. Seconds later he was cursing both himself and the person who had invented the device.

As she walked down the hall toward the bedroom April could hear the low, indistinct rumbling of Quinn's voice. At least she wouldn't be waking him, she thought. But before she could knock, the door was suddenly opened.

The sight of Quinn with only a towel around his waist caused her heart to skitter to a halt, and all coherent thought to flee from her mind. Her breath became trapped somewhere between her lungs and her throat, and as she stared at his lean, muscular body, a strange sensation began to uncurl somewhere deep inside her.

He looked roguish, his wet hair shiny and in disarray, and the dark stubble of beard outlining his jaw gave him a decidedly unkempt appearance. Though there were still faint circles under his eyes, he looked relaxed, rested and totally devastating.

She had seen men in skimpy bathing suits before, but looking at them had never elicited the kind of response that was struggling to life within her now. A flush spread slowly over her face and for a moment she was tempted to turn and run.

'April.' Quinn's gaze traveled over her, noting the pink tinge of color that was creeping delicately over her cheeks. 'Just the person I need. I'm having trouble with the lock on my suitcase,' he explained. 'I'm all thumbs today. Could you help?'

'Of course,' April said, hoping she sounded as casual and unaffected as Quinn appeared to be.

'I can't get the numbers lined up,' he said as he stepped aside to let her enter. With a nervous smile, April crossed the threshold, wishing her heart would slow its frantic pace. 'The numbers are six, eight and two,' he told her as she crouched by the suitcase.

Concentrating hard, she turned the tumblers on both locks to the numbers he'd mentioned, all the while acutely aware of the man standing nearby. With a click the suitcase opened.

'Thank you,' Quinn said with a smile.

'You're welcome,' she replied automatically as she stood up. Turning, she found herself only inches away from him, her eyes directly in line with the dark hollow of his throat. Her pulse took another giant leap as she noticed the bronze hair curling on his chest.

'Now I can get dressed,' Quinn said

and he moved past her.

April released the breath that had momentarily been trapped in her lungs and headed for the door. 'You must be hungry. I'll fix you something.'

'Fine, but you — ' Quinn began, but his words were lost on her as the door closed. Taking fresh clothes from the suitcase he began to get dressed. As he undid the towel from around his waist, a smile slowly began to curl at the corners of his mouth.

He couldn't recall ever before seeing a woman blush at the sight of his partially clad body, but she had indeed been blushing. What other explanation could there be for the way the delicate color had risen to her cheeks, giving a fragile innocence to her face?

Most of the women he knew would have smiled seductively and then made a pass. But April's embarrassment had been real and he found this appealing.

For the past eight years he'd been living and working in an environment where innocence was an attribute few people laid claim to. He knew his cynicism was due to the fact that his work and his life were surrounded by the glamor, glitz and hype that were part and parcel of the superstar syndrome.

But superstardom and all it meant had long since lost its appeal. Not that he hadn't enjoyed and appreciated his success — far from it — but during the past year he'd become restless and dissatisfied with the direction his life had taken. On reflection, he'd discovered that the road he'd traveled had brought him more rewards and satisfaction than had attaining his goal.

And more recently, he'd all too often experienced this feeling of discontentment, of disillusionment. Perhaps in this quiet corner of the world he'd have time to take stock of his life, time to ponder on just where he was going. But first and foremost, for his own peace of mind he had to find out what happened during those hours prior to the accident. He firmly believed that before he could face the future he had to understand the past.

* ★ ★

In the kitchen April was cracking eggs into a bowl. As always when she was upset, anxious or nervous, she found that preparing food had a calming effect on her.

She began by beating the eggs into a frothy yellow foam, to which she added a good pinch of salt and a measure of milk. Her movements were mechanical, controlled, while her thoughts revolved around Quinn and the stunning impact his near-naked presence had had on her.

He'd seemed completely at ease and totally oblivious to the fact that all he wore was a towel. She, on the other hand, had found herself dealing with an emotion that was both new and a little frightening.

He was beautiful. It was as simple and as complex as that. She'd never thought of a man's body as beautiful before. And certainly, she'd never experienced the overwhelming desire to reach out and touch him, to feel the texture of his skin and explore those muscular curves. Dear heavens! Her hand grew still for a moment before resuming its efforts with renewed vigor. Was what she'd experienced the physical attraction she'd read about in books, but never believed existed?

No! She quickly denied the thought. Her reaction, she told herself calmly, rationally, was entirely due to the fact that the body belonged to Quinn Quartermain, actor and celebrity; the man countless women admired, dreamed about and yearned to meet.

'April?'

At the sound of his voice, April spun around, almost dropping the bowl.

'I didn't mean to startle you,' Quinn said apologetically.

'That's all right,' April murmured, trying desperately to gather her scattered wits. 'Do you like scrambled eggs?' she asked, turning to pour the mixture into the pan on the stove.

'Yes,' Quinn replied. 'But please, I don't expect you to wait on me.'

She turned to him, noting the way his jeans hugged his thighs and the rust-colored sweater outlined his broad shoulders. His hair, several shades darker than the sweater, was dry now but still unruly, falling over his forehead in a highly captivating style. Dressed or undressed, his body was indeed beautiful. April felt the telltale warmth begin to spread over her face once more. Abruptly she turned back to the stove, stirring the eggs aggressively. 'This is ridiculous!' she muttered under her breath.

'Did you say something?' Quinn asked, moving closer.

'No, nothing,' April said. What on earth was happening to her? Why did she suddenly feel as nervous and as awkward as a teenager who finds herself alone with the most handsome boy in the class? 'Won't you sit down?

The eggs will be ready in a few minutes,' she heard herself say in a stilted tone.

Quinn complied with her request. He was aware of her nervousness, but didn't understand the cause of it. He turned his attention to the scene outside and instantly found himself absorbed by the view. The waters of the bay were less than a hundred yards away, and stretched towards a horizon that was totally undefinable because of the choppy surface of the ocean. 'Fantastic!' he murmured, drinking in the power and beauty that were spread invitingly before him.

'Yes, yes, it is,' April agreed as she placed a plate of eggs on the table in front of him. 'I never tire of the view. It's always different, and always the same,' she added, her voice generating a warmth and love she made no attempt to hide.

The appetizing aroma of the eggs turned Quinn's attention to the food. 'You make a mean scrambled egg,' he said a few moments later, smiling at her.

'Thank you.' She was unaccountably pleased with his compliment. 'Would you like coffee?' she asked, bringing the carafe to the table.

'Mmm . . . Please,' Quinn said, glad to see that she appeared more relaxed now. 'I'd just like to tell you how grateful I am,' he began as he reached for the cup of coffee she'd poured. 'Not everyone would be generous enough to invite a stranger into their home.'

'But you're not really a stranger,' April said. She returned the carafe to the stove, then joined him at the table. 'Besides, Greg would never have forgiven me if I'd said no.'

'Greg?' Quinn studied her face for a moment, wondering if Ian had forgotten to fill him in on the fact that April had a husband or lover. The thought made him frown.

'Greg's my younger brother,' she explained. 'He's nearly fifteen and one of your biggest fans.' She smiled, recalling Greg's reaction to the news that Quinn had arrived.

Fascinated, Quinn watched the smile as it gently made its way over her features. She had a quiet, uncomplicated beauty that she seemed unaware of. Just looking at her, Quinn felt something as yet undetermined stir within him.

'I hope Greg won't be a problem,' April continued. 'I'll try to keep him out of your way,' she added, casting a brief but anxious glance in his direction. Honey-gold eyes met hers and for the second time in less than an hour April felt as if the breath had suddenly been knocked out of her. She could hear her heart pounding in her ears and wondered if Quinn could hear it too. Did he have this effect on every woman? she wondered, as she fought to regain control of her senses.

'There's no need for that.' Quinn's words broke the silence and the spell. 'Besides, I'm the one who should keep out of your way.'

April made no comment, at a loss to understand why one look from Quinn should affect her so profoundly.

'I guess you're right when you say we're not strangers,' Quinn went on. 'I hope you didn't forget my advice about staying away from underground parking garages.' His words were followed by a smile.

The simple fact that he remembered sent a delicious thrill of pleasure through her. She returned his smile, totally unaware that her expression reflected her pleasure, openly, honestly and quite beautifully.

'I haven't been able to avoid them altogether,' she told him. 'The apartment block in Seattle where I live has one. The security there is good. That's one of the reasons I chose it.'

'It seems a shame that that kind of security is necessary,' Quinn commented, wishing she'd smile again. Her eyes had looked cool and yet exciting, like the depths of the ocean on a hot summer day.

'I know,' April said, her expression serious now. 'It seems that nothing — ' She stopped abruptly as she recalled the stranger she'd seen earlier. 'Oh! I completely forgot about the man outside.'

'What man?' Quinn was instantly alert, like a soldier who is suddenly called to attention.

'I was coming back from a walk along the beach when I saw a truck pull into the driveway,' she explained. 'At first I thought it was a neighbor, but the driver seemed more interested in Ian's car, and when — '

'Ian's car?' Quinn cut in.

'Yes,' she went on, puzzled by the sudden tension in him. 'When he opened the car door, I yelled and started to run, but by the time I reached the cabin he'd gone.'

'Did you recognize him?' he asked, his tone urgent now.

'I wasn't close enough to get a good look,' April said, surprised by his intensity.

'Would you know him again?'

'I'm not sure . . . No, I don't think so. He was too far away. I wondered if he might have been a reporter.' April voiced the thought that had passed through her mind earlier.

'I doubt it. A reporter would have stuck around,' Quinn commented, dismissing the idea. 'Besides, no one but Ian knows I'm here.' He was silent for a long moment, willing himself to remain calm. 'The car probably looked like an easy target,' he continued. 'Some thieves these days have nerve enough to walk into a house while the owner is at home and steal from under their noses.'

April nodded, remembering her mother had recounted a similar incident that had happened last summer. The culprit had turned out to be a teenager whose family had been camping at the state park.

While his explanation was plausible, April was not altogether convinced that it applied in this case. The drastic change in Quinn the moment she'd mentioned the stranger had been alarming. And she'd heard a note of desperation in his voice when he'd asked if she would be able to recognize the man.

She knew by the intense expression lingering on his face and the faraway look in his eyes that something was troubling him.

Studying him now, she saw both pain and frustration in the golden depths of his eyes — and found herself fighting the urge to reach out and soothe the pain away.

5

Someone had followed him!

Even as Quinn gave April an alternative explanation, he knew without a doubt that his fears had been confirmed. He broke out into a cold sweat. Who was it? Who had taken the time and effort to follow him from Los Angeles? And more importantly, why?

Quinn was suddenly filled with a deep sense of frustration. The stranger had to have something to do with Sasha's death. Damn! Why couldn't he remember?

'Quinn?' April spoke his name softly. He seemed to be off on a distant planet and from the expression on his face, what he found there was causing great distress.

She wanted to help, wanted to erase the lines of pain and worry from his face. 'Quinn.' She spoke his name again and this time was unable to control the impulse to touch him. Reaching across the table, she covered his hand with her own, unprepared for the tingle of awareness that accompanied the touch.

'Hmm?' Quinn suddenly found himself staring into a pair of hazel eyes filled with tender concern. 'I'm sorry, April. I was miles away.'

April said nothing; she was waiting, foolishly hoping that he would confide in her.

When his gaze dropped to where their hands lay, Quinn suddenly felt the desire to pour out his fears. There was something warm and comforting about the touch of her hand. When was the last time anyone had ever touched him in a simple gesture of caring?

Quinn brought his gaze back to her eyes, seeing again the genuine concern for him expressed in their depths. 'I know this will sound strange,' he began, 'but — '

The sound of a car door slamming startled them both. April was the first to recover. As she withdrew her hand, she almost groaned in frustration. Quinn had been on the verge of telling her something important, she could sense it, and now the moment was lost.

'It's Greg,' she said, and as if her words were a signal Greg burst through the front door. At the sight of Quinn seated at the kitchen table, Greg came to an abrupt halt.

'Wow! Like, holy Toledo!' he said, his eyes wide.

'Greg!' April scolded her brother. 'Where are your manners?'

'What?' Greg glanced at his sister, then back at Quinn. 'Oh, yes . . . Hello. I mean, nice to meet you,' he mumbled.

'Nice to meet you, too,' Quinn said, getting to his feet. 'I'd offer to shake hands, but it's too painful an exercise for me right now.' Quinn held up his right hand, revealing the plaster cast.

'That's okay,' Greg said politely, then burst out: 'You look kinda different with that mustache and beard. For a minute I thought it wasn't really you, but your voice — I'd know your voice anywhere,' he continued, his tone reverent.

'I'll take that as a compliment,' Quinn said, lowering himself into his chair once more.

Greg grinned, and dropped into the chair beside Quinn. 'Are you going to make another movie with the character Dirk Freeman?' he asked earnestly and without preamble. 'That was the best spy movie ever. Dirk was like another James Bond but more realistic,' he hurried on, 'and I thought at the end when one of the president's aides managed to slip through the net that the whole thing was being set up for a sequel.'

'Greg.' April put a hand on her brother's shoulder. 'Quinn is our guest and I don't think — '

'Please,' Quinn interrupted. 'It's all right.' The smile he gave her was heartwarming. 'I don't mind. In fact this kind of feedback is really helpful. Who better to talk to than a member of the teen audience these movies are generally geared toward?'

Greg glanced at his sister, his smile widening, a glint of amusement in his brown eyes.

'Be warned!' April said good-humoredly. 'He'll pester you with questions until you'll want to gag him with something.' She tried to sound severe, but failed.

As she moved away Quinn noticed a flash of something on her left hand. Instantly he focused on the small diamond and ruby ring on the third finger. The ring had to signify an engagement, he reasoned, a fact that left him feeling strangely deflated. He should have noticed it before, of course, but he'd been too wrapped up in himself.

To cover his momentary lapse, Quinn quickly turned his attention to Greg. 'You're right about the sequel, Greg,' he told the youth, 'but as yet I haven't seen a script that comes close to the first.'

'Now that you're directing, I didn't

think you'd go back to acting,' Greg commented.

'It's not unusual these days to do both,' Quinn said.

'Right. Wow! Do you think that one day you might do a sequel to *Deception Runs Deep*?' Excitement colored his voice.

'If the right script comes along.'

'Some of the action scenes were totally awesome,' Greg said. 'Did you do your own stunts?'

'I did most of the stunts in my earlier movies, but when I broke my leg during a race sequence in *Scorpion Sunrise*, the director insisted I stop.' Quinn smiled at the memory.

'You mean you worked even though your leg was broken?' Greg's tone was incredulous.

'Shooting was delayed for a couple of days until I was able to hobble about,' Quinn explained.

'I guess they couldn't wait until the break healed,' Greg said, leaning forward to rest his forearms on the table.

'No, but luckily we managed to finish the project without further mishap.'

During the discussion, April had been at the sink washing carrots and broccoli for the evening meal. Like Greg, she had been hanging on Quinn's words and throughout the conversation found herself liking him more and more as he patiently answered Greg's questions.

She turned from the sink to take pork chops from the refrigerator and her gaze caught Quinn's. For a breathless second she felt as if she were adrift on a vast ocean, captured by the warmth and the laughter she could see in his eyes.

'Did the stunt go wrong?' April heard Greg's voice somewhere in the distance, and only when Quinn turned back to answer Greg was she able to break free of the trance she found herself in.

April didn't hear Quinn's reply. She was too deep in her own thoughts, trying once again to understand what it was about him that seemed to reach out and somehow hold her captive.

He was only a man, after all. Handsome to be sure — perhaps more so than most — but that alone didn't account for the fact that each time she found herself looking into his eyes, it was as if he were gently nudging to life some secret inner part of her she hadn't known existed.

'Hey, April, did you hear that?' Greg's excited voice broke into her musing.

A smile on her face, she turned to survey the twosome at the table.

'Quinn says he'll teach me some of the basic moves he uses to do stunts!'

'Great,' April said, 'but first I suggest you make a few moves of your own — toward your room and the homework waiting for you there.'

'Homework! Ugh! What's that? Never heard of it.' Greg flashed a grin at Quinn.

'Hmm . . . Well, let me explain,' April said. 'Homework is linked closely to food.' She tried hard not to smile at the look that appeared on Greg's face.

'Homework and food!' he echoed. 'How can that be?'

'The equation is a simple one,' April continued, warming to the topic. 'If homework is not completed, then food will not be served.'

'That sounds very much like blackmail to me,' Quinn said in a conspiratorial tone, enjoying the teasing rapport between brother and sister.

'I think you're right,' Greg agreed. 'What should my strategy be?'

'I would suggest you withdraw to your room to consider the matter more carefully.'

'A good idea,' Greg conceded. 'But on one condition,' he added as he faced his sister.

'Let's hear it,' April said, knowing full well what the condition would be.

Laughter lurked in Greg's eyes. 'Ah, one apple and two scones?' came the tentative reply.

April couldn't stop the smile his words induced. 'Granted.'

Greg quickly commandeered what he'd bargained for and with a shrug of his shoulders headed for his room.

April smiled at the retreating figure, then turned to open the can of cream of celery soup and pour it over the pork chops. She placed the dish in the oven, then arranged the potatoes alongside.

Silently Quinn watched her complete the task. Her movements were quick and efficient and full of confidence. The promise of beauty he'd seen years before had indeed been fulfilled, he thought as he studied her.

She wore no makeup, and there was a natural glow to her skin that drew his gaze. Her hair had been brushed and tamed once more, but Quinn was recalling the windswept disorder of those soft curls, the color of which reminded him of rich dark walnut. Long thick lashes protected eyes that changed hue to mirror her emotions, and for a fleeting second, Quinn found himself wondering what color passion would be.

Annoyed with the turn of his thoughts, he reminded himself that she wore another man's ring. That man would one day be her husband, and even now most probably was her lover.

Suddenly he found himself remembering the way she'd blushed earlier, and instinctively he knew that her reaction had been a reflection of herself — honest and innocent. She was a woman untouched, her passion, her sensuality yet untapped. As this thought flitted through his mind, he was surprised to experience both admiration and envy.

Of the two, admiration was somehow easier to understand. Who could help but admire a woman who, during these controversial times, had held fast to her own beliefs and was true to herself? But envy? How could he be envious of a man he'd never met?

'I did warn you.' April's voice brought him back to reality.

'Warn me?'

'That Greg would talk your ear off,'

April said as she gathered the dishes from the table.

'And I did say that I don't mind,' he affirmed. 'Besides, I like him. I hope we can be friends.'

April's hands grew still, and she glanced at Quinn. Seeing the sincerity in his eyes, her heart turned over. Why couldn't David have said those words? But unlike Quinn, David had found Greg's straightforward manner annoying and abrasive.

'Thank you,' she said.

'For what?' he asked quietly. 'He's easy to like.'

The dishes momentarily forgotten, April straightened and focused her attention on a seagull bobbing on the water just offshore.

'It's just that I worry about him. A sister's privilege, you know,' she added, tossing Quinn a smile. 'Though he doesn't say much, I know he misses his father. We both do,' she amended, suddenly finding herself blinking back tears. 'But I've always felt that Greg misses him most. He and Dad were very close. They were always off sailing or fishing. Or they'd be watching the Seahawks and occasionally they'd go to a Mariners' game. Mom would tease them, calling them Sports Incorporated.' April stopped. Her throat was tight, and the tears filling her eyes threatened to spill over.

She waited, watching the gull lift off the water with a flutter of wings and a splash. 'It's been tough on him,' she said, almost to herself.

'I'd say it's been tough on you, too,' Quinn replied softly, fighting the urge to get up and pull her into his arms.

April shook her head. 'I'm sorry. I don't know what got into me. I didn't mean to unload on you like that.' She forced a laugh, and began to gather the dishes once more, moving to stack them in the dishwasher.

'There's nothing to apologize for,' Quinn said, rising from his chair.

April made no comment. How easy it had been to voice her concern for Greg.

With David, any mention of the boy only served to create tension between them, so she had refrained from talking about her brother. Though this had bothered her considerably, she was at a loss to know how to change things.

Something she'd read years before came to mind. *Sad but true*, the heading had read. Beneath it was a discussion of the fact that some people could talk to strangers, expressing quite eloquently their innermost hopes and fears, yet were unable to share them with the person most dear to them.

'I think I'll unpack,' Quinn said, breaking into her wandering thoughts.

'Supper will be ready in an hour,' she told him, glad of the chance to be alone. Quinn had only been there for a few hours, yet she couldn't help feeling that she'd known him for a lifetime. The notion was troubling, to say the least.

★ ★ ★

The evening meal was one of the most pleasant experiences Quinn had had in a long time. The food was delicious, and the two people seated at the table with him made him feel so totally at home that he could almost believe he was one of the family.

Only when he visited Ian, Jane and the boys did this feeling of contentment emerge, but over the years those times had become both infrequent and all too brief.

There was so much warmth, so much love inside these walls that he found himself wishing he could hold on to this moment and make it last forever.

Throughout the meal Greg continued to slake his seemingly inexhaustible thirst for knowledge about Quinn's career. Quinn found the questions and remarks made by both Greg and April interesting, intelligent and sometimes thought-provoking.

'Will the movie you were working on ever be released?' asked Greg. 'I mean — because of the accident.'

April threw her brother a startled look. Quinn had been relaxed throughout the meal, but at Greg's words the tension she had seen the previous night dropped over him like a veil, erasing the warmth from his eyes and causing a shiver of apprehension to chase across her skin.

'I think you've asked enough questions for one night, Greg.' April spoke quietly, filling the yawning silence.

'No . . . it's all right,' Quinn said, following his words with a smile that did not quite reach his eyes. 'Actually, I'm not sure what will happen,' he told them truthfully. 'But I do know that it would be a crime if the public were denied a chance to see . . . Sasha's performance.'

April heard the brief hesitation and closed her eyes against the tortured look that came into his eyes.

The warm atmosphere they'd enjoyed throughout the meal had suddenly vanished, leaving in its wake a rather pensive mood that no one seemed eager to dispel. Greg, too, had nothing more to say.

A few minutes later, Quinn rose from the chair. 'Dinner was delicious, thank you. I'm rather tired. If you'll excuse me, I think I'll turn in. Good night.'

'Good night.' April and Greg spoke in unison and watched as Quinn walked down the hallway to his room.

'Help me clear the table,' April said, propelling herself into action and trying not to think of the expression on Quinn's face when he had spoken Sasha's name.

'I guess you're mad at me,' Greg murmured as he reluctantly stood up. 'I'm sorry, April. I just got carried away.'

April stopped what she was doing and turned to her brother. 'Greg, I'm not mad at you. It was inevitable that the conversation would at some point turn to the accident or Sasha Gray.'

'Do you think Quinn's angry at me?'

'No, I don't,' she told him truthfully. 'He's still dealing with his grief. It was an awkward moment, that was all. There'll probably be more of them, but they'll get easier. Now forget about it and help me load the dishwasher.'

★ ★ ★

Quinn slid the patio door open and then drew a deep breath of sea air. The darkness was soothing. The cool breeze caressing his skin was almost like a lover's touch, and as he watched beams of light dance across the water he felt the muscles in his neck slowly begin to relax.

His rather abrupt departure from the table had bordered on rudeness, but he'd suddenly found himself unwilling to face more questions about Sasha, and the conversation seemed destined to head in that direction.

He usually tackled problems with a strong determination to overcome them, using the maximum of efficiency and the minimum of time. He'd never been tempted either to ignore a problem or to put it aside, but now he found himself in a situation where his usual approach was impossible.

Until his memory returned he was a prisoner of his own mind, and his anger and frustration were caused by the knowledge that he was powerless to do anything about it.

With a sigh, Quinn turned and went inside, sliding the door shut. Still dressed, he stretched out on top of the bed and closed his eyes.

The sound of someone knocking on the bedroom door woke him instantly. Glancing at his watch he saw that it was only nine o'clock. He'd been sleeping for little more than an hour.

'Come in!' he called, swinging his legs off the bed to sit on the edge.

Greg poked his head around the door. 'I hope I didn't wake you,' he said. 'Ian's on the telephone. April told me to tell you.'

'Thanks, Greg,' Quinn said, rising and moving toward the door. Greg withdrew, then disappeared into his own bedroom. When Quinn reached the living room, he found April seated in an armchair, the phone at her ear.

'He's here, Ian. Just a minute,' April said. With a quick, agile movement she was out of the chair, holding the receiver toward him.

As Quinn accepted it he was faintly aware of being enveloped by the sweet scent of spring flowers, and as their hands touched he had an impression of softness and silk.

'Hello Ian,' he said, faintly distracted.

'Hi! You made it!'

'You had doubts?' Quinn asked, amusement evident in his tone as he lowered himself into the chair April had vacated.

'No,' Ian said, then laughed. 'But I just wanted to make sure. You had no trouble then?'

'Nothing,' Quinn said, without the least hesitation. His suspicions were still unconfirmed and though there had been the incident with the car, it would take more than that to warrant bringing the police into the matter.

'Great. Everything is quiet here. I called in on Robson tonight on my way home and he's playing his part in the scheme. There weren't as many reporters parked outside your house this time — they must be losing interest in the story.'

'That would be a welcome change,' Quinn said.

'Oh, and I checked with the detective as you suggested,' Ian went on. 'He told me the police will release a more extensive report on the accident by the end of the week.'

'I want you to send me a copy.'

'Of course. I'll mail it express to April — that should get it there overnight.'

'Thanks, Ian. I really appreciate all you're doing,' Quinn told his friend.

'What are friends for? Listen, Jane sends her love. Ah, I imagine it's too soon to ask, but any progress?'

Quinn was silent for a moment. 'No, nothing,' he answered.

'I assume you haven't told April about

losing your memory,' Ian continued.

'What purpose would that serve?' Quinn asked as his gaze slid to where April sat in the kitchen reading the newspaper.

'I'm not sure,' Ian said. 'Sometimes it helps to have someone to talk to. Well, I'll keep in touch. Call me if you need anything.'

'I will.' Quinn replaced the receiver, his expression thoughtful as he recalled that he'd come very close to telling April the story that afternoon. The urge to confide in her had been strong indeed — and more than a little surprising.

Throughout his life he'd been wary of women, unwilling to let himself grow too close. The reason he'd found it difficult to trust them had to do with the fact that his mother hadn't wanted him. She'd married his father, a budding young artist, believing that fame and fortune were but a short step away. When these did not materialize within the first year, she became disillusioned with her husband and dissatisfied with their marriage, though by then she was pregnant. Then, shortly after the birth of her son, she'd packed her things and walked out, leaving her husband to cope on his own.

Somehow they had managed. Though not always orthodox in his methods, Evan Quartermain had given freely of his love, taking Quinn with him wherever he went.

What little he made from the watercolors he painted was used to buy food, and only when he found a permanent job, working in a small theater company painting scenery, did their lives become more stable. Quinn would accompany him to the theater every chance he got, and would sit for hours watching the actors and actresses rehearsing. It was there his ambition to become an actor was born.

His father's death seven years ago in a boating accident had been a tough blow for Quinn. After the funeral he had been grateful for the fact that he was starting work on a new film. He had thrown himself into the project — working long hours in an attempt to keep the pain of his loss at bay.

It had been nearly a year later, when he had dropped in to visit Ian, that he had found himself pouring out his feelings about his father. Jane and the boys had been with their grandparents, leaving Ian at home alone. Over a dinner that Ian had cooked, they'd consumed two bottles of a vintage cabernet Quinn had brought — and suddenly he had found himself talking about his father — remembering, reminiscing. And as he talked a sense of peace returned.

Yes, Quinn thought, talking things out was certainly a valuable way to come to terms with problems and emotions. What he found disturbing right now was the realization that he had indeed been about to confide in April, and no doubt would have done so, had Greg not arrived. He was beginning to trust her.

6

'Is everything all right?' April's voice broke through Quinn's thoughts, and he looked up to find her standing by the chair.

'Fine . . . fine,' he repeated, as if to convince himself. As he stood up, the flowery fragrance she wore seemed to tug gently at his senses and for a moment he felt the sweet murmurings of desire stir within him.

He grimaced in annoyance at this reaction and watching him, April felt sure that his expression was caused by pain.

'Is your arm hurting?' she asked, concern evident in her voice. 'Would you like some aspirin?'

'No, it's nothing,' he said, suddenly feeling foolish. Seeing the puzzled look on her face, he added an abrupt 'Thanks.' She really was quite beautiful, he thought distractedly, but with none of the affectation or pretension of the women he usually came in contact with. Perhaps that was the reason he'd never allowed himself to become deeply involved with any of the women he had costarred with or directed. He'd had brief, casual relationships throughout his career, but no one woman had ever managed to touch his heart. He wasn't sure he even believed that true love existed. Only when he visited Ian and Jane and saw the evidence of their love for each other did he find himself wondering if one day he, like Ian, might be lucky enough to find his own soul mate.

April was finding it difficult to break away from Quinn's thoughtful gaze. Her skin grew warm under his scrutiny and her heart was suddenly galloping as if it were trying to escape. She was captivated by the bemused expression in his eyes.

He was going to kiss her! The thought flashed into her mind, causing her heart to stop in midbeat.

'I'll say good night again,' she heard Quinn say in a husky voice. Without waiting for a reply, and as though he couldn't wait to leave, he moved past her and on down the hall to the guest room.

April felt as if she had suddenly been dipped in ice-cold water. Her body was shaking, and it was several moments before she was able to still the trembling.

She'd been so sure he was going to kiss her, and the disappointment she felt was overwhelming, to say the least. What was the matter with her? She was engaged to one man, yet she was eager to kiss another? It was with this troubling thought that April retired to her room.

★ ★ ★

April was surprised when Quinn wandered into the kitchen early the next morning. Greg looked up and smiled a greeting and April, as she popped more bread into the toaster, wondered at the way her heart seemed to trip over itself before resuming its normal pace.

She turned from the counter in time to see Quinn pour himself a cup of coffee, then join Greg at the table. He wore a long-sleeved pale blue shirt, unbuttoned at the sleeves and rolled back to reveal the plaster cast on his arm. Dark blue jeans hugged lean hips and thighs, and for a moment April found herself recalling those moments the previous day when all he had been wearing was a towel. Annoyed with the turn of her thoughts she banished the image from her mind, and tried to concentrate on the sandwich she was making for Greg.

'What's on your agenda today, Greg?' she heard Quinn ask.

'School.' The word was more like a grunt. Greg's tone conveyed a great deal.

'I gather you're not particularly fond

of school,' Quinn said.

'It's okay . . . sometimes,' said Greg with a shrug of his shoulders. 'I just wish I didn't have to go there every day,' he added, casting a glance at his sister.

Quinn smiled. 'I know what you mean,' he sympathized.

'But unfortunately you do,' said April, setting the toast on the table for Quinn. 'In fact, you have to leave in five minutes.'

'Maybe after school I can show you some of those moves I was telling you about,' Quinn said, and was rewarded by seeing Greg's face light up.

'Would you?'

'Of course, but only if you promise to show me the best fishing spots around here.'

'All right!' Greg was on his feet. 'Thanks Quinn, you've got a deal. Now I'd better get out of here or I'll miss the bus. See you later.'

'You bet,' Quinn said, before turning his attention to the toast.

'Thank you,' April murmured as she refilled his coffee cup.

'For what?' Awkwardly he tried to spread jam on a piece of toast. 'Damn!' he murmured as the jam fell off the knife and landed on the table.

'I'll do that,' April said, moving to take the knife from his hand. As their fingers touched she felt a tingle of awareness race up her arm. Surprised, she drew away, wondering a little at her response.

'It's amazing all the little things you take for granted,' he commented ruefully after she'd finished. He bit into the toast and April sat down in the chair Greg had vacated. 'By the way,' Quinn continued a few moments later. 'I noticed a small sailboat alongside the cabin. Is it seaworthy?'

April smiled. 'You must mean the good ship *Lollipop*,' she said. 'Yes, it's seaworthy. My father built it for me,' she explained, her tone softening.

'Would it be all right if I took her for a sail?' he asked. 'Mind you,' he added with a rueful grin, 'it's been a while since I did any sailing.'

'She's fairly easy to handle,' April told him, 'but you might have trouble, especially with your arm out of commission.'

'Hmm . . . You're right,' Quinn said thoughtfully.

April could hear the disappointment in his tone. 'I could go with you . . . I mean . . . that is, if you don't mind company.' She ground to a halt, her fingers nervously fiddling with the saltshaker.

'Terrific!' Quinn replied enthusiastically. 'But are you sure? I don't want to take you away from anything important.'

'I'm working on some sketches, but they're not urgent,' she told him, the idea of sailing with Quinn becoming increasingly appealing.

Quinn sipped his coffee. 'Sketches? Ian said you were part owner of a boutique. Are you a designer too?'

'I design wedding gowns,' April

explained. 'My friend Bobbi and I run a bridal boutique.' She was unable to hide the pride in her voice.

For the next hour April found herself telling Quinn about the boutique and how her dream had become reality. He was a good listener, genuinely interested in her accomplishments, and his questions and comments sparked a lively conversation. It was April who glanced at the clock on the kitchen wall and saw that it was almost ten-thirty.

'Good heavens, look at the time!' she exclaimed. 'And I haven't cleared the breakfast dishes away.'

'Let me help,' Quinn said, rising to his feet. 'When we're done, if you haven't changed your mind, we can go for a sail.'

'You're on,' April said, and as her eyes met his a warm glow of pleasure spread through her.

It was obvious as they worked together that Quinn had no qualms about helping her, and she found herself admiring the fact that he actually seemed quite at home in this domestic scene. What she found disturbing was the way Quinn's presence somehow seemed to dominate the kitchen, a room she had always considered large and spacious.

As she finished wiping the sink she found herself thinking of David, recalling the times she had cooked dinner for him at her apartment. Generally the meals she'd produced on those occasions had taken both time and effort. David had been complimentary and appreciative, but he'd never offered to help clean up. After dinner he always carried his coffee into the living room and then called to her to join him.

'Do you keep the mast and sail in the garage?' Quinn's question broke into her thoughts.

'Yes,' April said. 'Everything should be there. In fact I know exactly where they are. I had to move them the other day before I could get my car in.'

Quinn was quiet for a moment.

'Would there, by any chance, be room in the garage for Ian's car?' he asked. 'That way it would be out of sight . . .' His voice trailed off.

'No problem,' April assured him, realizing that he was thinking of the incident with the stranger. 'We can switch it with mine.'

Quinn accepted her suggestion, appreciating the fact that April did not question him about his request. When the cars had been moved he helped her carry the mast, sail, rudder and centerboard as well as two life jackets to the waiting boat. Soon the *Lollipop* was ready to go.

'It's nearly lunchtime,' April said. 'I'll make a few sandwiches to take with us. I don't know about you, but sailing always makes me hungry.'

'That sounds like a good idea,' Quinn agreed as they made their way up the beach to the cabin. 'Is there anything I can do?'

'You'll need a jacket or sweater,' April said. 'It'll be pretty cold out on the water. I can manage in the kitchen, thanks.'

When Quinn returned a few minutes later, April was waiting for him at the door. She was holding a brown paper bag that contained several chicken sandwiches, two apples and a small thermos with the remainder of the morning's coffee.

Quinn climbed into the boat and sat at the stern. As he settled in position, he drew a deep breath, exhaling slowly, savoring the feeling of excitement, of exhilaration that was taking command of his body. He couldn't remember the last time he had taken time simply to do something he enjoyed. And it was April he had to thank, he thought as he watched her push off, then jump in to take her position at the bow.

Neither spoke as they worked together to set the *Lollipop* on a course across the bay. To their mutual surprise and pleasure, they found they worked well together, almost as if they had always been sailing partners, and as the sail billowed to capture the cool November breeze they glanced at each other and smiled.

As the *Lollipop* skimmed across the water, April gloried in the feel of the wind kissing her face and tugging at her hair. The waves splashed against the boat and the tangy fragrance of the sea surrounded her. Her eyes met Quinn's once more and she felt her pulse skip crazily.

'Where to, Captain?' he asked in a teasing tone, laughter dancing in the golden depths of his eyes.

'We could head for the village marina,' she suggested, pointing to the land to the starboard side. 'Whitehorn Point is at the opposite end of the bay and is in the direction we're headed.' April tried to keep her tone light but wondered if she was successful — her heart was behaving very erratically whenever she glanced at Quinn.

'Then Whitehorn Point it is,' Quinn replied. 'Though to tell you the truth I wouldn't care if we were heading for

Hawaii.' With a smile he stretched his long jean-clad legs before him. 'I'd completely forgotten how being out on the water can give you a feeling of utter freedom, as if you'd escaped from the world. There's nothing like it.'

April nodded. Whenever she'd needed some time alone away from everyone, she'd gone sailing. Manning the boat usually commanded all her concentration and energy, leaving no room for anything but the sheer joy of living. She'd come back rested and rejuvenated, ready to face the world again.

She was surprised to find that Quinn's emotions reflected her own and she was surprised, too, that this knowledge should bring her the pleasure it did.

April issued instructions to Quinn, who was manning the rudder. It took over an hour to reach the headland and during that time several motorboats crossed their path, their occupants waving as they passed by. April's stomach was beginning to rumble, and she was glad she had taken the time to pack a lunch.

Throughout the journey Quinn had asked questions about the area and obligingly April had answered them. But during the silences that ensued she felt no need to talk or chatter and fill those peaceful moments with inconsequential words.

She suddenly realized that if David had been with her she would have felt compelled to fill the quiet times. He was a man who was always in a hurry, rarely content to take time out to sit and quietly savor the simple joys of life. Actually, it was ridiculous to even imagine David relaxing in a sailboat; he preferred to feel the power and speed of an engine beneath him, whether in a motorboat or a car.

April frowned. What was the matter with her? It seemed that each time David intruded into her thoughts she found herself comparing him with Quinn.

She glanced at the man opposite her.

Quinn, his left hand on the rudder, was leaning back looking totally at ease. His eyes were closed but April doubted that he was asleep. Long brown lashes fanned cheeks that were smooth till they reached the fringes of his beard. She continued her scrutiny, taking in the sculpted planes of his strong cheekbones, and the strength and character of his bearded jaw and chin.

Her eyes came to rest on his mouth and the fainter dusting of his mustache, which served to accentuate the firm line of his lips. She felt a strong urge to reach out and touch him, to discover for herself whether his beard was as soft and sensual as it looked.

A feathery feeling, like the whispery touch of a caterpillar tiptoeing across her hand, suddenly caught at her heart. She felt breathless and totally bewildered by these sensations that were slowly quivering to life within her. How could simply looking at a man create these strange murmurs of desire?

When his eyelids flickered open,

April looked away and drew a ragged breath, wishing she felt more in control. She shook her head, as if to deny that she was feeling anything at all, and turned her attention to the distant shoreline, concentrating on locating the cabin they had left behind. After a moment, she shifted her gaze to Quinn, only to experience that now-familiar jolt to her senses.

'Hungry?' she asked, marveling that her voice sounded normal.

'Ravenous,' came the reply, as he adjusted his position on the hard wooden seat.

April opened the bag and pulled out the thermos, setting it on the boards at her feet. Plunging her hand into the bag again she brought out the sandwiches and handed one to Quinn.

'Rats!' she murmured under her breath, realizing she had omitted to pack an extra cup.

'Not in the sandwiches, I hope,' Quinn said, a look of mock surprise on his face.

April saw the glint of amusement lurking in his eyes and a bubble of laughter quickly surfaced and broke free.

The sound was like music. Watching her, Quinn found himself responding to the joyful notes, his own laughter joining hers.

April shook her head, trying to ignore the warmth, the feeling of closeness that had suddenly sprung up between them. 'They're chicken sandwiches,' she told him, trying, without success, to stop smiling, 'but next time . . . ' she added in a threatening tone. 'Next time, beware!'

'Next time,' Quinn echoed, enjoying the exchange, mesmerized by the dancing lights in eyes that were impossibly green, 'I shall put myself in sole charge of food.'

'You, sir, have a deal,' April said with a flourish, and at the expression on Quinn's face she broke into renewed laughter.

'Why do I have the feeling I've just

been outsmarted?' he asked, before biting into his sandwich.

'Would you like some coffee?' April asked a couple of minutes later.

'Coffee sounds great.' Quinn tossed the plastic wrap into the brown bag at his feet. 'The sandwich, by the way, was delicious,' he continued as he accepted the thermos lid April had half filled with steaming coffee. 'Aren't you having any?' he asked a few moments later.

'I forgot to put in another cup,' she explained, shaking a strand of hair away from her face. 'I'll have some when you're finished.'

'Nonsense! Here, have a sip.' He held out the lid and reluctantly she took it, her fingers brushing against his, sending a frisson of heat up her arm.

Her hand was shaking ever so slightly as she brought the cup to her mouth. All she could think about was the fact that his lips had also touched the rim somewhere. It was ridiculous that this thought should create such a tremor inside her, but there was no denying that it did.

She sipped the coffee, which had quickly cooled, fanned by the sea breeze. She took a second sip just as a wave caused by the wake of a passing motorboat reached them. As the sailboat crested the wave, April gave a gasp of surprise as the liquid spilled over her mouth and down her chin.

Quinn reacted quickly, reaching forward to take the cup from April's hand, cursing himself as he did for not having noticed the wave, for not warning her.

'Did you burn yourself? Are you all right?' he asked urgently, concern for her overriding his good sense. He made a move to stand up, an action that caused the sailboat to list dangerously.

'Stay there!' she ordered. 'I'm fine, really. The coffee wasn't very hot. I'm okay,' she repeated and breathed a sigh of relief as he resumed his position.

'I'm sorry,' Quinn said. 'I should have warned you.' But he'd been too busy staring at the slender curve of her neck and the pulse beating at the base of her throat, imagining how her skin would feel beneath the tender caress of his mouth.

'Accidents happen,' she said and immediately wished she'd used another phrase — for at her words, he seemed to withdraw. An expression of grief touched his features, bringing lines of anguish and pain to his face. Pain and something more . . .

What was it? How she wished she could ask him! But whatever demons Quinn was wrestling with, he chose to face them alone.

Quinn leaned back against the hard surface of the boat, annoyed with himself for reacting to what, after all, was a perfectly innocent remark. She was puzzled, and had every right to be, he told himself. But the look of sympathy and understanding he could see in her eyes touched him deeply.

Undoubtedly whatever April knew about the accident was what had been reported on television and radio. And while the police had absolved him of all responsibility, the media had not been kind in their comments. He wasn't at all sure he would ever be able to rid himself of the feeling of guilt that haunted him — but he could see no accusation, no condemnation in her eyes. Her gaze held only compassion and caring.

What he couldn't shake was the feeling that there was something out of place about the whole affair. And until he could recall the circumstances leading to the accident — until he could resolve the questions in his mind — he knew he would never be able to rest. Suddenly, for the second time in as many days he found himself wanting to confide in April, to tell her of his suspicions, his fears, everything.

His brows drew together in a frown and for a moment he wasn't sure what troubled him more — his loss of memory or the growing need to talk to April about it.

Quinn suddenly realized that the

boat's movement had changed from a gentle bobbing to a rather more energetic dance, and glancing around he noticed they had passed the headland and were in the open waters beyond the bay.

Thankfully he realized that his hand had remained steady on the rudder; his preoccupation could well have created a dangerous situation. If he'd been on his own, his lapse might have proved disastrous.

He glanced at April and the sight of her calm, intent expression helped the tension seep out of him.

'I was miles away,' he confessed, his tone serious. 'I'm sorry.'

The apology surprised her and yet somehow gave her the courage to say the words that had been hovering on her lips since she'd seen his expression change.

'Tell me. I'd like to help.' Her words were carried to him on the breeze, and were expressed with such sincerity and sensitivity that they reduced his already crumbling resistance to zero.

The frustration, the anger and the fear came pouring out. 'I don't remember anything. Sasha's dead and I don't remember how it happened.' The agony in his voice caught at her heart. 'They told me I wasn't at fault,' he went on, his voice rising in anger, 'but how can I be sure that's true, when I can't remember a damned thing about it?' He drew a ragged breath and when he continued, his words were precise and controlled. 'Maybe the reason I can't remember is because I'm afraid to face the truth — that I was responsible — that I killed Sasha.'

'No!' April's gasp was whipped away by the breeze. To have survived such a terrible accident and then awaken to the news that someone you loved had died would be devastating indeed, but to awaken and discover you remembered nothing would be horrifying.

Her heart ached for him, and though she longed to offer comfort, she knew mere words would do little to ease the pain he was inflicting on himself. But the fact that he had unlocked the door to that pain, that he trusted her enough to share it was akin to being given a precious gift.

She inhaled and tried to steady the rush of her heartbeat. No, Quinn was not the kind of man to seek sympathy from her or from anyone else. What he needed was someone to help him deal with the situation, help him come to terms with his feelings of frustration and guilt.

'I don't believe for a moment that you're responsible,' she told him firmly. 'And when your memory returns you'll know that, too.'

Surprise brought his eyes to hers, and as she boldly held his gaze he saw that she meant every word. Her belief in him was unquestionable, and for the first time since awakening to the nightmare he felt as if the heavy load he'd been carrying had been made lighter.

April glanced at her wristwatch,

hoping to hide the telltale color that suddenly flushed her face. 'Perhaps we should head in,' she suggested, and for the next few minutes as they set a course for home they were quiet, each with their own thoughts.

'What do you remember?' April asked as they tacked toward the shore.

Quinn sighed. 'I remember arriving in L.A. I remember doing the talk show that night. I even remember leaving the studio and walking to my car.'

'And Miss Gray, was she with you?'

'Yes. I was going to give her a lift back to her apartment.'

'You drove to her apartment . . .'

Quinn grimaced and closed his eyes, trying to remember. An image of Sasha flashed into his mind, but it was of the mischievous smile she'd thrown his way when the interviewer had asked her a question about her relationship with Quinn.

There was no relationship, of course, but Sasha saw no reason to make a public denial. Right from the outset she'd seen that an association with him was a way to keep her name in the limelight and help to further her career. At every opportunity she'd blatantly added fuel to the rumors that were circulating about them.

He'd been annoyed at first, but discovered that Sasha had an inherent streak of mischief and fun, so it was difficult to be angry with her for long.

But wait . . . Another image of Sasha flashed briefly into his head, but this time her expression was one of alarm, and he could see fear in her eyes. His heart stopped, and his breath caught in his throat. He tried to tell himself his memory was playing tricks, simply supplying him with a scene from the film. But there had been no such scene and as this fact registered, he could feel the hairs on the back of his neck begin to rise. Desperately he tried to hold on to the image, which had already begun to fade.

'Quinn . . . Quinn!'

His eyes flew open at the sound of

April's voice, and the breath he had been holding escaped in a rush. 'Are you all right?' she asked. 'Your face went so white.'

'I remembered something,' he said, hardly able to believe it himself.

'That's wonderful!'

'I didn't drive to Sasha's.'

'Where did you go?' April asked.

'I . . . I don't know.' Quinn's tone had changed. The excitement was gone, replaced once more by impatience and frustration.

'It's beginning,' April said, wanting to hug him and shake him at the same time. 'As the old cliché goes — Rome wasn't built in a day.'

Quinn smiled in spite of himself. 'How long did it take?' he asked, feeling himself relax, wondering fleetingly how April had so easily reduced the tension that had been building within him.

'I haven't the foggiest,' she told him, turning to see that they were nearing the shore. A gathering of sea gulls flew off in a flurry of noise as the boat sailed toward them, and nothing more was said.

April had already pulled up the centerboard and as the boat scraped against the rocky sea bottom, she readied herself to jump ashore. Landing safely, she turned and heaved with all her strength to bring the bow out of the water.

The boat rolled and shifted under his weight as Quinn unsteadily made his way toward April. He held his arm against his body, which made it difficult for him to maintain his balance. As he stepped clumsily onto the bow, the boat began to tip, unbalancing him completely.

Quinn made a futile attempt to grab the mast to stop his fall, but his fingers merely brushed the wood in passing. His grunt of warning was wasted and his body collided with April's, sending the two of them sprawling in the sand.

April couldn't move; she couldn't breathe. Quinn's left arm held her pinned down. It had happened so quickly that she'd had no time to react. She wasn't hurt, only winded. She took a couple of quick breaths and started to move, but hadn't got far when Quinn lifted his head and she found herself staring into the amber depths of his eyes.

'Are you all right?'

His face was barely inches from her own. As his breath fanned her face, a tingling awareness began first to creep across her skin and then spread quickly throughout her body. One part of her mind urged her to move, to get away, while another pressed her to close the gap between them.

The decision was taken from her as Quinn lowered his mouth to hers.

April's world suddenly began to spin, the stars whirling around and through her creating a heat so intense that she thought she must explode.

She'd never known a kiss like this. Just the tickle of his mustache sent sparks through her, igniting a need that set her on fire. Her hands reached for and found the silky smoothness of his hair, reveling in the feel of it. He was drawing a response she hadn't known she was capable of giving.

Quinn struggled to regain control of emotions that were spiraling ever higher within him. Her skin held the delicate fragrance of primroses and pansies and she tasted of the wind and the sea. Her lips were so incredibly soft and yielding that he wondered for a moment if he were dreaming. But when her mouth opened beneath his, the flash of desire that splintered through him told him it was no dream.

Never before had he experienced this sudden, dizzying need. His tongue gently probed the sweet moistness of her mouth and he wanted nothing more than to touch, to stroke, to explore the exquisite sweetness that was April.

Almost roughly he drew away, tearing the web of passion that threatened to entangle him, stunned to discover that one kiss could propel him so quickly to the edge of reason. His breathing was ragged as he looked down at her delicate features. Her lashes flickered open, and he almost forgot his resolve when he saw the desire simmering in the depths of her eyes.

Dazed, April stared at Quinn for several seconds. During those moments when he had kissed her, she had been drawn into a world of sensation, into a world that she had never traveled before. Now, as Quinn moved away from her and stood, she was filled with a strange sense of loss as if somehow he'd taken some vital part of her with him.

When he offered her his hand she hurriedly scrambled to her feet, brushing the sand from her jeans and giving herself time to gather her composure.

'April . . . I'm sorry.'

'Please, it's all right,' she said, wishing her heart would cease its frantic pounding. She raised her eyes to his but found she was unable to meet his gaze. Instead she glanced over his shoulder — in time to see the sailboat start to drift away from shore.

'The boat!' she exclaimed, moving past him to grab the trailing rope. As she pulled it in, she found herself thinking that Quinn's devastating kiss had set her own emotions dangerously adrift as well.

7

Quinn was silent as he helped April haul the boat onto the beach and all the way back to the cabin.

In the sanctuary of his room, he leaned against the door for several moments, trying to make some sense of his jumbled thoughts and emotions.

Why had he kissed her? What in heaven's name had prompted him to do such a thing?

Quinn pushed himself away from the door and raked a hand through his hair. He began to pace the small room, fumbling with his sweater until he managed to pull it off. He threw it onto the bed and continued to pace.

It had been an impulse he simply hadn't been able to resist. Then why was he pacing the room? Why was he feeling so wound up? It was only a kiss.

He stopped in front of the small oval

mirror that hung on the wall and stared thoughtfully at his reflection. Yes, one kiss was all it had been, but somehow that kiss had burned its way to the very core of his being, leaving him feeling strangely vulnerable.

And if the sudden rush of desire the kiss had ignited surprised him, then the aching tenderness that accompanied it had been infinitely more puzzling.

He'd kissed her, that was all. Quinn strode to the sliding glass doors and stood gazing at the ocean. He tried to convince himself that nothing had changed, but a tiny voice inside his head kept telling him that nothing would ever be the same again.

★　★　★

In the kitchen April seasoned and browned the pot roast she had taken from the freezer earlier that morning. With quick, deft movements she sliced potatoes, carrots and onions and arranged them around the meat, finishing off by adding a little water.

As she worked her mind was replaying the scene on the beach. His lips had touched hers so very gently, and the delicate caress of his mustache had sent a delicious thrill along her nerve endings. He had seemed content to simply taste and explore, but with a tantalizing skill that drew an eager response she could neither control nor deny.

Why had she allowed the kiss to happen? She could have avoided it. She *should* have avoided it.

April glanced at the ring on her left hand and with great deliberation turned her thoughts to David. All she could think of was that David's kisses had never elicited the kind of response that had flared to life the moment Quinn's mouth had touched hers. What was happening? What did it mean?

April tried to concentrate on the ingredients needed for the cheesecake she'd decided to make for dessert, determined not to let her thoughts dwell any longer on those moments at the beach. After all it was only a kiss. A brief . . . casual . . . *devastating* kiss. Stop it! Annoyed with herself, she tossed the spatula she'd been using into the sink.

As she was sprinkling cracker crumbs over the top of the dessert, Greg came in. April's greeting was lost as he slammed the door behind him, then disappeared down the hall to his room.

April set the finished dessert aside and frowned. Something was wrong. Perhaps now was as good a time as any to have a chat with him, she decided, making her way to Greg's room.

She knocked and waited, then hearing a grunt from within, slowly opened the door. 'Have a bad day?' she asked as she sidestepped the clothes and records strewn on the floor. Greg was not the tidiest teenager. His room resembled the aftermath of a tornado, but both April and her mother had long since refused to feel responsible for a mess not of their making.

'You could say that,' Greg said. He was lying on top of his unmade bed.

'Want to talk about it?' April asked as she bent to pick up a book that lay open on the floor.

'What's to talk about? School's a bummer.' Greg rolled away from her to face the wall.

'Mind if I sit down?'

'Help yourself,' came the mumbled reply.

April sat on the end of the bed, wishing she knew where to begin. 'Greg, something's obviously bothering you, and if there's anything I can do, I'd like to help. I'm a pretty good listener, you know,' she added in an encouraging tone.

Greg rolled onto his back, then sat up. He seemed about to speak, then, with a shrug of his shoulders reached for his desk to pluck an envelope from one of his schoolbooks. 'Here!' he said, holding the envelope toward her.

April glanced at her brother but his expression told her nothing. She

160

opened the single sheet of paper inside and read:

Dear Mrs. St. Clair,
Would it be convenient for you to come to my office tomorrow morning at nine? I wish to discuss a matter that concerns your son. If this time is inconvenient, perhaps you could call the office and make another appointment.

Reginald Brandon
Principal

April read the note a second time, then looked at her brother. 'What's this all about, Greg?'

'Are you going to go?' he asked.

'Of course,' April said, trying hard to keep the exasperation out of her voice.

'You'll find out then,' Greg replied, hugging his knees and avoiding her gaze.

'Agreed,' she said. 'But I'd like to know what it's about before I get there. Come on, Greg. This isn't like you. I want to help, but I can't unless you tell me what's going on.'

There was a long silence, which Greg broke at last. 'Mr. Brandon's already made up his mind,' he said. 'So it won't make any difference what I say.'

'It makes a difference to me,' April said quietly.

Greg sighed and placed his chin on his knees. 'There's a guy at school who keeps bugging me, that's all.'

'What do you mean, bugging you?' April asked, sensing that his attempt to make light of the situation was perhaps an indication there was more beneath the surface.

'Look, it's nothing. I can take care of it.' Greg moved off the bed and stood at his desk. He reached for a pencil and began tapping it against the table.

April folded the note and returned it to the envelope. 'Who *is* this guy, and how long has he been bugging you?' she asked.

Greg threw the pencil into the air, caught it, then turned to face her. 'He's new at school. He's in my math class. His name's Frankie and he's a bully and a creep.'

'I see,' April said.

'Look, Sis, I appreciate what you're trying to do, but I've got to figure this out by myself.'

April nodded, knowing he was right. To have her intervene would merely make matters worse, especially in the eyes of his peers. April felt a stab of sympathy for Greg. The problem was a tough one and she was sure he'd been carrying the burden of it for a while, possibly since the start of the term.

'I understand what you're saying, but I need to know what happened to bring Mr. Brandon into the picture.'

Greg sighed. 'I was standing by my locker, minding my own business, when Frankie came up behind me. He grabbed me and started to shove me into the locker. I was struggling pretty hard but he just kept laughing. I guess a crowd gathered and it was getting noisy. Frankie must have seen Mr. Brandon coming because he suddenly let me go and as I turned to take a swipe at him, Mr. Brandon was standing right there. Talk about timing!' he finished with a groan.

'Hmm . . . ' April nodded and smiled ruefully. 'But surely if Frankie's a troublemaker, Mr. Brandon would know about it.'

'Frankie's pretty good at making things look innocent — he gets away with a lot. Like I said, he's a creep.'

'Bullies are basically cowards,' April said, 'that's why they pick on someone smaller.' She sighed and rose from the bed. 'I'm not much help, am I? But at least I'll be prepared for Mr. Brandon tomorrow. Thanks for filling me in.' April gave Greg a pat on the shoulder. 'Supper will be ready in about an hour.' She turned and left the room, closing the door behind her.

April returned to the kitchen and stood looking out across the bay. She felt angry at the youth who was making Greg's life difficult, and wished there was something constructive she could do. What would their father have advised? she wondered. A wise and gentle man, he might have been able to suggest a more definite course of action. April sighed.

'Something smells good.' Quinn's voice cut into her thoughts and she tried to ignore the leap of her pulse at the sight of him.

'It's pot roast,' April said, surprised that her voice sounded so matter-of-fact. 'But it won't be ready for another hour,' she added, moving away from him to open the dishwasher.

'Did I hear Greg come in?' he asked.

'Yes, you did. He's in his room,' she told him as she began to put away the clean dishes. She opened a cupboard door and when she turned around, Quinn was holding a glass out for her.

'I can manage,' she told him, wishing suddenly that he wasn't so helpful or considerate, then perhaps she wouldn't find herself liking him quite so much.

'Let's just say it's my way of saying thanks for going sailing with me today.'

'I couldn't let you go alone,' April said, meeting his gaze — and wishing seconds later that she hadn't. He had the most fabulous eyes of any man she'd ever seen. A strange weakness suddenly invaded her body and she almost dropped the plate he'd handed her.

'It felt wonderful to be out on the water. I hadn't realized how much I've missed it,' she heard Quinn say. 'We made rather a good team, don't you think? Maybe we could try again tomorrow. I could use the practice, especially when it comes to landing,' he added, and April heard the hint of humor in his tone.

She turned away, carefully placing the plate on the shelf, trying to quell the butterflies that had suddenly taken up residence in her stomach. He was deliberately making light of the kiss, and she supposed she should be glad, but instead she felt a stab of pain somewhere near the region of her heart.

Quinn cursed under his breath. He hadn't meant to say anything about those moments on the beach — in fact he'd advised himself to forget the kiss altogether. An easy task, he'd thought. But his resolve had quickly evaporated the moment he'd seen April staring thoughtfully out at the ocean, looking as though the world were resting heavily on her shoulders.

His impulse then had been to pull her into the shelter of his arms, but he'd managed to control it. The flash of pain he'd just seen in her eyes surprised him and indeed had almost been his undoing. Dammit! For the first time in his life he felt like a teenager on his first date, undecided whether to kiss her or shake her hand.

'I can't go sailing tomorrow,' he heard April say. 'At least not in the morning,' she amended. 'I've been summoned to the principal's office.'

'Not for skipping school to go sailing with me, I hope?' he teased gently.

April laughed softly. 'No, actually it's about Greg.'

'Hmm, that sounds ominous,' Quinn said. 'Surely Greg isn't in trouble — he doesn't strike me as the type.'

April's hands grew still for a moment. She raised her eyes to his. 'You're right, he isn't,' she said, then smiled, warmed by the sincerity she could see in his eyes. 'It would appear that he's become the target for a new guy in school who likes to push people around.'

'Ah!' Quinn said softly, wondering at the sudden erratic behavior of his pulse. He felt sure it was reacting to the smile she had bestowed on him.

'I just wish I could do something,' April said, anger creeping into her voice. 'But he has to work this one out on his own.'

'Try not to worry,' Quinn advised, reaching out to touch the silky softness of her hair. 'Things have a way of sorting themselves out.' His knuckles gently grazed her cheek and as his hand made contact with its satiny smoothness he again felt the swift rush of desire that had roared through him on the beach.

His heart began to beat wildly as he was enveloped by the flowery scent that was hers alone. He felt suspended in time, held captive by a pair of eyes that were regarding him with undisguised gratitude. Inch by inch he drew closer to the mouth that seemed to be trembling in anticipation, waiting to be joined by his.

He was trembling too, as his mind, body and senses came alive with a need so powerful that it robbed him of coherent thought. Yet running parallel with his desire was a wistful kind of longing . . . a longing for something more . . .

'Hey, April, if supper — whoops!' Greg came to a halt.

Quinn and April sprang apart like two kids caught with their hands in the cookie jar.

'Hi, Greg,' Quinn said, forcing a

smile, when in fact he wanted to groan in frustration.

'Hi,' Greg returned, then flashed his sister a speculative glance. 'I came to get an apple,' he said, moving to the refrigerator.

'Help yourself,' April told him in a voice that wavered slightly. She stepped to the sink, putting some distance between herself and Quinn, surprised by the disappointment that was washing over her. She'd wanted Quinn to kiss her, wanted to feel his mouth on hers, to experience those delicious sensations his kiss could arouse so quickly and so easily. She turned on the tap, letting the cool water flow soothingly over skin that was decidedly warm.

'Do you have much homework tonight?' she heard Quinn ask Greg.

'No. Actually, I'm almost finished.'

'Great,' Quinn replied. 'After supper we can get started on a few of those moves I was telling you about. They come in handy in all sorts of ways.'

'Terrific,' Greg exclaimed.

April turned in time to see the two of them leave the kitchen, each munching happily on an apple.

*   *   *

'Is it all right if we push back some of the furniture in the living room?' Quinn asked after the supper dishes had been cleared away.

'Of course. Just put everything in its place when you're finished,' April said.

'Are you going to watch?' Greg asked, his face alight with anticipation.

'No, I'll leave you to it. I have a few phone calls to make,' April said, heading down the hall to her mother's bedroom.

Bobbi answered on the first ring.

'April! How are you?'

'I'm fine. How are things at the boutique?'

'Quiet. Teresa Santini is due in for her final fitting tomorrow. I just hope she doesn't decide on any last-minute changes,' Bobbi said, her tone doubtful.

'The wedding's on Saturday and you know what she's like.'

'Don't remind me,' April said.

'I'll let you know how the fitting goes,' Bobbi assured her before ringing off. April replaced the receiver and sat thoughtfully for a few moments, listening to the sound of laughter coming from the living room. Resolutely she dialed David's number, giving up only after she'd repeatedly encountered a busy signal.

When she emerged from her mother's bedroom, she could still hear Quinn's deep voice. The rich tones of their shared laughter drew her to the living room, and when she saw Greg sprawled on the rug, a smile curled the corners of her mouth.

'Good. Now try that again,' Quinn instructed. Greg hopped to his feet, preparing himself once more.

'Tuck your head in and roll. Try to relax.'

Greg did as he was bidden, landing rather less awkwardly this time. April moved further into the room and sat down on the reclining chair, which had been pushed back out of the way.

Her respect for Quinn steadily increased as he patiently coached Greg through a number of moves and countermoves. Watching them together brought a warmth to her heart, and emotion tightened her throat. At fourteen, Greg had reached a point in his life when the friendship, love and support of a father or older brother would indeed be valuable. Quinn, with unquestionable ease, had readily stepped into the breach. Somehow April couldn't picture David on his hands and knees on the floor helping Greg, and at this thought a feeling of sadness descended on her.

Not for the first time April found her thoughts disturbing. Surely, if she loved David, then she would simply accept the fact that he was a man of a different character. But somehow she couldn't help thinking that if she truly loved David, she would not be viewing his differences as shortcomings.

The telephone beside her rang, breaking into her thoughts. She reached for the receiver. 'Hello.'

'April? Is that you?' The line crackled, then cleared.

'Mother! How are you? How was your flight?'

'Lengthy, but wonderful,' Laura St. Clair said. 'I just wanted to call and make sure everything was all right.'

'Everything's fine, Mother. Greg is right here — I'll let you talk to him in a minute. How's Aunt Frances? What's the weather like in Auckland?'

'The weather is quite warm. It's summertime here and the flowers are so lovely. Aunt Frances is fine and sends her love.'

'Hold on, here's Greg.' April rose from the chair and handed the receiver to her brother, who was hovering nearby.

'Mom! Yes, I'm fine. April's not as good a cook of course, but that's okay.' He laughed, successfully ducking a playful punch she sent his way. Greg talked for several more minutes, then handed the phone back to April.

'I forgot to ask her what time it was in New Zealand,' Greg said. 'Don't you lose a day or something traveling west?'

Quinn nodded. 'When you cross the date line going west you add a day, going east you subtract a day.'

'I'll get my atlas. Then we can figure out what time it is there.'

'Hold it!' April said, replacing the receiver. 'If the two of you are finished here, perhaps you could return the room to its original form?'

'Slave driver.' Greg grinned, then moved to do as April had asked.

When the phone rang again moments later it was Greg who reached for it. 'Hello!' he said cheerfully, then the smile slid from his face. 'It's David,' he announced and held the receiver toward his sister. 'Come on, let's get out of here.' he said to Quinn. 'April will want to be alone. David's her fiancé.'

Quinn found it somewhat difficult to keep his expression neutral, for Greg's words had caught him off guard. As he turned to follow Greg, he wondered about the youth's change of expression the moment he'd identified the caller. It was obvious that Greg didn't think too much of his sister's fiancé — a feeling Quinn suddenly found himself totally in agreement with.

'I called you earlier, but your line was busy,' April said.

'I was talking to Brian at the office,' David replied. 'Well, what's new with you?'

'Not a great deal,' April said, relieved to note as she turned that she was alone. 'How about you?' she asked, trying to put a little enthusiasm into her voice.

'I'm in the final stages of putting together the pictures and story on those teenage runaways,' David answered with more than a hint of pride. 'I've got a couple of new ideas I'm working on, but I'm still hoping to get an interview with Quartermain, if he ever comes out of hiding.'

'What do you mean 'out of hiding'?' April asked, trying to sound casual, when in fact she was holding her breath as she waited for David's answer.

'Well, he's still refusing to talk to anyone. Says he wants to wait until the accident report is released. In the meantime I've been putting together a file on Sasha Gray. By all accounts they were one hot couple. Rumor had it they were heading for the altar.'

April's grip on the telephone suddenly became painful. She knew she had no right to care whether Quinn had been in love with Sasha Gray or not, but somehow the statement brought with it an acute stab of . . . what? Could it be jealousy?

That night April lay awake for a long time, trying to sort out her feelings. Before she finally drifted off to sleep, she told herself that she must try to maintain a distance from Quinn, wondering all the while if the dull ache

David's news had evoked would ever go away.

★　★　★

April awoke to the smell of coffee brewing. She flung back the covers, grabbed her robe from the foot of the bed and hurried to the kitchen.

'Good morning!' Quinn turned from the stove and smiled at the surprised look on her face. His heart skipped a beat as he lazily let his gaze travel the full length of her. That she had just awakened was obvious by the disheveled appearance of her hair, the robe that lay open to reveal a nightdress the color of a ripe peach and feet that were bare. 'I hope I didn't wake you,' he began, trying, without success, to keep his eyes away from the creamy-white skin that was visible above the V neck of her nightgown.

'No,' April replied as she self-consciously drew the edges of her robe together, wondering all the while why

178

her skin should suddenly feel as though it were on fire. He looked devilishly handsome. It was the only word she could think of that accurately described him. He was wearing black denims and a short-sleeved, black T-shirt that was molded to his upper body like a second skin. The white plaster cast on his right arm simply accentuated the outrageous good looks.

Nervously her hand went up to smooth her hair and as she raised her eyes to meet his, a new and utterly devastating sensation began to uncurl somewhere deep in her abdomen. Her mouth felt dry and her heart seemed to be beating out a rhythm that echoed throughout her entire body.

It was incredible; without even touching her, Quinn could elicit a response that left her body quivering with expectancy!

Quinn watched in total fascination as her eyes turned an exquisite shade of green. The desire he had felt stir within him at the sight of her became almost impossible to contain. She was a witch! She had to be! And the spell she was weaving around him was like nothing he had ever known. He wanted her! Yes! With an intensity that frightened him. But he was not altogether sure that, having once possessed her, he would ever be able to let her go. And he was forgetting one very important fact — she was engaged to another man.

With an effort, he clamped down on emotions that were threatening to overpower him. 'Are you hungry?' he asked, his voice husky. He cleared his throat. 'I'm attempting to make French toast. It used to be my specialty, but it's taking me a little longer than usual,' he added with a rueful smile. 'Would you like some?' He turned away from her to the bowl on the counter.

'Sounds great,' April said, her heart faltering a little. Did he have any idea how devastating he looked when he smiled? she wondered. Each time she encountered another aspect of this man, she found her resolve melting away like the butter in the frying pan. 'What time is it?' she asked.

'Seven.'

'You're up early.'

'I couldn't sleep,' Quinn answered. 'I went for a walk along the beach. Thought it might help.'

'Is something wrong?' she asked, unable to hide the concern in her voice.

He glanced over his shoulder as he dropped a piece of bread into the mixture. 'Only a headache,' he said, playing down the throbbing pain that had kept him awake most of the night. 'I feel better now,' he lied.

April studied him for a moment, this time seeing the pain in his eyes. She wished with all her heart she could do something to ease it.

She moved toward him, then, as if thinking better of it, she stopped. 'I'd better shower and get dressed,' she said.

'Breakfast in five minutes,' Quinn announced, as April disappeared from view.

When April returned to the kitchen

ten minutes later it was to find Greg seated at the table, deep in discussion about one of the stunts Quinn had performed in the movie *Deception Runs Deep*. Quietly she accepted the plate of food Quinn held out to her, listening to his detailed explanation of how carefully the stunt had been planned and choreographed.

As she sipped the coffee Quinn placed before her, April noticed again the lines of pain around his eyes and mouth. Perhaps after she and Greg were on their way to school, Quinn would return to bed and catch up on the sleep he'd missed. And it was with this thought in mind that an hour later April ushered Greg from the cabin.

To her surprise, her meeting with Mr. Brandon turned out to be not at all what she'd expected. The principal informed April that he was well aware of the tendencies of Frank Baker to incite trouble. His reason for wanting to talk with her was, in fact, to acquaint her with the situation.

As she drove home, April felt a little more confident that Greg's problem, with the help of the school, might well be resolved.

It started to rain as she pulled into the driveway. Switching off the engine, April stepped from the car and hurried toward the cabin. The clouds above were darker now and promised more rain, possibly for the remainder of the day. As she rounded the corner of the cabin, she came to an abrupt halt. Peering through the big bay window was a man she did not know.

'Can I help you?' she asked, trying to keep the tremor from her voice. He'd startled her, that was all. But as the man straightened, an unaccountable shiver of fear chased down her spine, and with it came a vague feeling that she'd seen the stranger somewhere before.

'Hi!' The man smiled, but April noticed that his pale blue eyes were as cold and distant as the horizon. 'I knocked, but there was no answer,' he said, taking a step toward her.

'I've been out.' April forced herself not to step back. 'Is there something I can help you with?'

'Well, I was wondering if I could rent one of your cabins,' he said in a tone that was overly pleasant.

'I'm sorry, but we're closed for the winter months.' April was relieved that indeed she was telling the truth. 'Perhaps you can come back again in May,' she said, keeping her tone light and friendly, but all the while finding the man's presence decidedly frightening.

'Oh, I'll be back, all right,' the stranger said grimly. With a nod of his head he walked past her and disappeared.

Frozen by the menacing tone she'd heard in the man's voice, she couldn't move. For several seconds April stood in the shelter of the patio while the rain pattered noisily on the roof.

With trembling fingers she let herself into the cabin. Where was Quinn? That question was uppermost in her mind, but she wondered, too, if he had heard something and was staying out of sight. She unzipped her jacket and tossed it on a nearby chair.

'April?' Quinn appeared in the hallway, fully dressed, but looking as though he had just woken. He ran his hand over his face, wiping the sleep away, focusing on the pale features and the look of alarm in her eyes. 'What's wrong? What happened?' he asked, closing the gap between them.

8

'April! Is it Greg?' All signs of sleepiness gone, Quinn grasped her by the shoulders.

She shook her head. 'No.' Her voice was barely a whisper as she momentarily gave herself up to the warmth and comfort of Quinn's nearness.

'Then what?' he asked staring intently at her, relieved to see the fear in her eyes subsiding.

'I . . . There was a man outside,' she began hesitatingly. 'He was looking in the window. He . . . ' She broke off as the memory that had been eluding her suddenly returned.

'What man?' Quinn's tone was urgent, his grip on her shoulders tightening.

April looked him in the eye. 'I think it was the same man I yelled at the other day — the one looking into Ian's car!'

Quinn froze at her words. 'Are you sure?'

April nodded.

'Can you describe him?' Quinn asked, holding her gaze, his eyes revealing little of the desperation he was feeling.

'Yes, but I don't understand. Why do you want me to describe him?'

He studied her for a long, breathless second. 'I don't understand either,' Quinn said, simply and truthfully. His hands dropped to his sides. 'This will sound insane, I know,' he began, as his hand moved to massage the back of his neck, 'but during the drive from L.A. I couldn't shake the feeling that someone was following us.'

'Following you?' April repeated his words, staring at him in surprise. 'But who . . . why?'

'I don't know. I wish I did. Then maybe some of this would make sense.'

April heard the frustration in his voice, and suddenly she found herself filled with the urge to reach up and soothe away the pain she could see on his face. Her hand made contact with the softness of his beard in a gesture that was solely meant to comfort.

His hand covered hers, trapping it against his face. Gold eyes met green ones and April felt her bones begin to melt. She felt as if she were being pulled toward him by an invisible force and she struggled for control, fighting the tide of longing that swept over her.

She withdrew her hand and stepped back, breaking the spell that had wrapped itself around them, ignoring the conflicting messages her brain and body were sending.

She inhaled deeply and with each passing second felt a semblance of control return. 'He was tall, not quite six feet,' she began. 'His hair was light brown, almost blond, and he had blue eyes . . . pale blue eyes,' she amended, recalling their cold expression. She shivered.

Quinn saw her reaction and noted, too, that the look of apprehension had returned to her eyes. He cursed under his breath. He wanted to pull her back into his arms, offer the comfort she so readily and unselfishly had given him. But moments ago, when she'd reached up to touch him, he'd found himself filled with the desire to taste again the honeyed sweetness of her mouth — to lose himself forever in the haven of her arms.

Quinn drew a deep breath. 'How was he dressed?' he asked, forcing his mind back to the problem at hand.

'Ah . . . Jeans and a black down vest over a checkered flannel shirt,' she said, watching as his face creased in an expression of deep concentration.

Closing his eyes, Quinn tried to conjure up an image of the man April had described. A minute ticked by, then another. Nothing was familiar, yet something vague and uneasy crawled across his consciousness. How he wished he'd dozed off in the chair instead of on top of his bed. Then he might have heard the stranger wandering around outside and been able to get a glimpse of him. 'Damn!'

'Quinn?'

His eyes flew open and at the expression of tender concern on her lovely face, he felt something stir deep inside.

'I'm all right,' he assured her, all the while trying to pinpoint the emotion that was gently nudging at the edge of his consciousness.

'Did you remember anything? Do you know who he is?' she asked.

'No,' he told her dejectedly. 'And I'm beginning to think I'll never remember,' he added, running his hand through his hair.

'Don't say that,' April quickly chastised him. 'You mustn't give up hope.'

'If only I'd seen him — '

'But you didn't,' she interjected, wishing there was something she could say that would help him.

'Why is he following me? What does he want?' The questions hung in the air like a guillotine waiting to fall. 'Dear

God! I wish I knew . . . ' He sighed. 'I just have this feeling — this gut feeling — that he has something to do with the accident.' He stopped. What he was saying sounded totally bizarre, and he expected to see skepticism in April's eyes. But to his surprise, he saw a measure of understanding, if not belief, and warmth and joy spread through him.

When he'd agreed to Ian's suggestion, it had simply been as a means to ease the pressure and give himself a chance to recover from the trauma of the accident. What he'd found here had been a friendly, caring atmosphere and two people who'd quickly come to mean a great deal to him. They'd given him a sense of family, of belonging, and April's kindness and support had awakened an emotion he was as yet unwilling to analyze.

Suddenly a thought occurred to him that brought him up short. Was it possible that by staying here he was endangering April and Greg? The stranger might return. It was in fact highly probable.

'Perhaps I should leave,' Quinn said, voicing his thoughts.

'Leave! But why?' April's eyes were wide with surprise.

'What if he comes back?' Quinn asked. 'He's here because of me. If I leave, he'll follow.'

The thought of Quinn leaving tore at April's heart. 'You can't be certain of that,' she heard herself say. 'Besides, where would you go?' As she spoke, she tried to keep a tremor from her voice.

'I don't know — '

'You're beginning to remember things. Leaving now wouldn't solve anything and might even jeopardize your chances of regaining your memory,' April said evenly, though her heart was thudding in her breast.

Quinn studied her for a long moment. 'You're right. Perhaps I'm overreacting.'

April could feel the tension easing from her body. Quinn was staying, at least for the moment, and the rush of relief that accompanied this realization left her feeling strangely weak.

'I think I'll give Ian a call and ask if the accident report has been released yet. Who knows — maybe something will turn up there,' Quinn said, though his tone lacked conviction.

'Good idea. I'll rustle up lunch,' she added before turning away.

'April.' His voice was little more than a whisper, making her name sound like a caress, as if his fingers had gently traced a path down her spine. Her pulse skittered to a halt, and every nerve was suddenly tingling with life.

'Yes?' She could barely get the word out as she turned to him.

'Thanks.' The sincerity and emotion in his voice stole the remaining air from her lungs. An aching longing assailed her and the warmth that was rapidly spreading through her turned her knees to water. When his knuckles gently grazed her cheek it was all she could do to remain standing. She found herself wanting to bridge the gap between them, to know again the wonder of his lips, to sip again from the cup of desire.

Quinn drew closer, ever closer to lips that were quivering in anticipation. He could not recall ever being held in the grip of such a strong emotion. It was as if April had somehow reached inside and peeled away the layers of restraint he had so carefully built around his heart.

What was this emotion that wielded such power and made him forget the fact that she was engaged to another man? The question acted like a splash of cold water and his body tensed. With a strange mixture of regret and sorrow, he forced himself to take a step back.

April exhaled slowly, painfully, telling herself Quinn's withdrawal was not the cause of the throbbing ache in her heart. Dear God! What must he think of her? She had all but thrown herself at him. Hot color washed over her face and she quickly moved to the kitchen, to lean against the counter, waiting for her heartbeat to steady.

From the moment Quinn arrived, something undefinable had begun to stir deep inside her. During the short time he'd been at the cabin she had come to know him as a caring, compassionate and sensitive man, a man who had wakened in her emotions she had not known she possessed.

April drew a quivering breath and brought her thoughts to a halt. She tried to tell herself that what she was feeling was nothing more than sympathy. Quinn was from another world, a world he would return to all too soon.

Pushing aside her reflections, April slowly prepared lunch. She went through the motions of making sandwiches and hearing that Quinn was still talking on the telephone, she reached for the mixing bowl and flour. Five minutes later, when Quinn joined her, she was kneading pastry dough for an apple pie. Her skin tingled with awareness as he pulled out a chair and sat down to watch.

'Any news?' she asked, avoiding his gaze and keeping her attention on the rolling pin and pastry.

'No, nothing,' Quinn said as he watched her long skillful fingers arrange the dough and prepare to roll it. 'Ian says he'll call the minute he gets a copy of the report.'

April was silent as she continued working, placing the rolled-out pastry on the pie plate. Thoughtfully she trimmed the edges, concentrating for all she was worth on the simple task and trying to ignore the erratic beat of her pulse that was caused solely by Quinn's nearness.

The sudden jangle of the telephone cut through the silence. With a sense of relief she moved to answer its summons.

'April, it's Bobbi. Listen, I hate to bother you . . . '

'No bother! What's up? Wait, let me guess. Teresa's fitting — it was a disaster, right?'

'How did you know?' Bobbi's tone

was a mixture of relief and surprise.

April laughed softly to herself. 'Just a wild guess. Okay, tell me what happened.'

'She's still here. She's in the changing room, insisting she's lost five pounds and that the waistline has to be taken in. She hates the headdress and wants the veil longer. I'm at my wit's end, April. I could just — '

'Scream,' April supplied easily. 'I know exactly how you feel,' she sympathized. Teresa Santini had been a problem right from the start, continually changing her mind about the style of her dress. 'Ask Teresa if she can come in tomorrow. Tell her I'll personally see to any adjustments she thinks are necessary. I can be there by eleven.'

'You'll come? Are you sure? What about Greg?' Bobbi asked.

'I'll make arrangements for him to go to a friend's house after school.'

'If you're sure . . . ' Bobbi's tone was laced with relief.

'Go and talk to her now. I'll hold on,'

April said. She should have known Teresa would find fault with something.

'Teresa says she won't be able to come in until one o'clock,' Bobbi said when she returned a few minutes later.

'One o'clock is fine,' April assured her friend. 'I'll see you tomorrow then,' she added before replacing the receiver.

'Problems?' Quinn asked as she rejoined him.

'A nervous bride-to-be,' April explained with a smile. 'Unfortunately, I'm going to have to make a trip into Seattle tomorrow.'

'Would you mind if I came along for the ride?'

April swallowed her surprise and tried to quell the sudden leap of her pulse. 'Of course not,' she managed after a moment's hesitation.

Greg, however, found fault with the arrangements. 'Why can't I just stay overnight at Mark's?' he asked. 'His mother won't mind and that way you won't have to worry if you're late getting back.'

April had to admit that his suggestion made sense. 'Well, if it's all right with Mrs. Crawford . . . '

'Call her and ask,' came the prompt reply.

As Greg predicted, staying overnight at his friend's posed no problem. When April rejoined Quinn and Greg in the living room it was to find them once more in the throes of practicing moves and countermoves. Again April was struck by the patience Quinn possessed. When the time came for him to leave, she knew that she would not be the only one to miss him.

★   ★   ★

The morning brought gray clouds and the promise of rain, but as April waved Greg off to school, the weather was the last thing on her mind. The prospect of the two-and-a-half-hour drive to Seattle with Quinn caused a quiver of nervous excitement to quicken her heartbeat.

She had spent the last few minutes

trying, with only a minimum of success, to tuck several recalcitrant strands of hair into a smooth and elegant chignon. But somehow they refused to cooperate, resisting all her efforts to be captured and pinned.

Annoyed, she gave up the fight and concentrated instead on applying a stroke of blush and a faint touch of eye shadow. She wore a dress of dark green wool with a wide black leather belt, and a black wool jacket. As she lightly covered her lips with lipgloss, she frowned at her reflection, completely unaware of the stunning picture she made. The effect was a subtle hint of mystery and just a whisper of sensuality.

Quinn waited outside on the patio, watching a small flock of seagulls squabble over a morsel of food. When he'd invited himself along for the ride, he'd simply seen it as a possible way to confirm that the stranger was watching him. But as he waited for April he found himself acknowledging that there was another reason, one that had nothing to do with the stranger and everything to do with April.

She was like no other woman he had known. Her very presence was a balm to his soul. And the fact that she believed in him, believed that his memory would return and ultimately release him from his prison of pain and guilt, touched him deeply. Her unstinting support had gone a long way to ease the tension he'd been living with since he'd woken up in hospital. Her openness, her depth of caring for someone who was little more than a stranger, seriously undermined all his well-established defenses. For the first time in his life he was in danger of losing his heart.

April closed the cabin door and turned to find Quinn watching her. Her breath caught in her throat at the sight of him. He looked like a marauding pirate come off his boat to pillage and plunder! At this thought her heartbeat quickened and her blood turned to fire in her veins. Never before had merely looking at a man elicited the kind of response that was flaring to life within her.

He wore light gray pants, a matching shirt and a black sweater. Over his shoulders was a black and gray jacket with suede trim. Silhouetted against the ocean he was a picture of strength, confidence and startling good looks. Yet when she turned her gaze to meet his, she saw once more the vulnerability and the pain. Her heart went out to him immediately.

Quinn pulled a pair of dark glasses from his jacket pocket and put them on. 'Think anyone will recognize me?' he asked.

April continued her study, wanting to commit to memory the picture he made, telling herself it would be all she'd ever have of him. 'It's always a possibility,' she said at last. 'But with your beard and the glasses, I'd say it's unlikely.'

'Good,' came the succinct reply.

'Shall we go?' He moved to her side and together they walked to her car.

A fine drizzle began to fall as they drove toward the highway. Throughout the journey Quinn kept up a steady stream of conversation, asking questions about the local area and its history. The miles and minutes were quickly eaten up and April found herself enjoying the charm and quiet humor of the man beside her.

By mutual consent they refrained from talking of the stranger. Though April noticed Quinn periodically glance around at the traffic, she made no comment, unwilling to be the one to break the harmony.

'What are you going to do all afternoon?' April asked as she changed lanes, opting for the express lane that would bring them to the center of Seattle.

'I thought I'd wander around and get acquainted with the city. Sightsee a little,' he told her.

April changed lanes once more in

order to leave the highway. 'The boutique's only a few blocks from the monorail station. It takes you to the Seattle Center. You might want to take a look. That's where the World's Fair was held in 1962.'

'Sounds interesting. I might just do that.'

Minutes later April pulled into the small parking lot at the rear of the boutique.

'When do you expect to be through here?' Quinn asked as they walked the short distance to the front of the building.

'With luck, no later than five,' she replied, sending up a silent prayer that Teresa would, for once, cooperate.

'That should give me time to find my way back. Perhaps later you can give me a guided tour of your boutique,' he added and at his words April felt warmth spread through her.

She nodded, then watched as Quinn made his way down the street.

Inside, Bobbi greeted her with a

smile and a hug. 'I'm really sorry about this, April.'

'Don't be silly,' April said, 'I should have known Teresa would kick up a fuss and want some last-minute changes. While I'm here I'll check the mail and do a little paperwork,' she added and crossed to the small office at the rear of the store.

'Leanne Cruickshank's going to be here any minute for a fitting,' Bobbi announced. 'She can only stay half an hour, so I'd better get everything ready. I'll leave you to it,' she said and with a wave was gone.

April leafed through the mail on her desk. She'd only been away from the boutique a few days so there was no urgent business requiring her attention — nothing to prevent her thoughts from straying to Quinn.

She was convinced he was not to blame for the accident, but if his memory didn't return, he would have to live with the agony of never knowing the truth about Sasha's death. He hid his pain well, but there were times when she'd seen the haunted look in his eyes and she wished with all her heart she could do something to erase it. He must have loved Sasha very much. A swift pain stabbed at her heart. David had even said a marriage was imminent.

Her thoughts skittered to a halt. David! Dear God! She reached for the telephone and dialed David's office, more than a little disturbed to realize how easily she had forgotten him. He answered after the second ring.

'Darling! What a lovely surprise,' David said. 'Did you get bored with your babysitting duties and decide to call me?' he questioned in a teasing tone.

April pushed back a sigh of exasperation. 'No, I'm not bored,' she told him. 'Actually, I'm calling from the boutique.'

'What are you doing there?' he asked. 'And why didn't you tell me you were coming to town?' He sounded piqued.

'I'm sorry, David — Bobbi called in a panic. Teresa Santini was unhappy about her final fitting, so I decided I'd better arrange another one and supervise it myself.'

'I see. Well, why don't I pick you up later and we can have supper together?' he suggested.

'I can't. Teresa is coming in at one and I don't know how long I'll be. I'm driving back later tonight,' she continued, as her thoughts returned to Quinn.

'How about lunch?'

'Lunch would be fine, but I do have to be back at one,' she said.

'Beggars can't be choosers, as the old saying goes. Give me half an hour and I'll meet you at the usual place.'

'Great!' April said, trying hard to infuse some enthusiasm into her voice.

* * *

April was the first to arrive. As she waited at the table by the window, she sipped thoughtfully from the glass of water the waiter had provided.

It was only a matter of minutes before she spotted David coming toward her, looking tall and handsome in navy slacks, a pale blue shirt and a tweed jacket. Watching him approach, she found herself waiting expectantly for her heart to skip a beat, as it was wont to do whenever she saw Quinn. However, its rhythm never faltered.

Her smile was forced as David bent to kiss her. She held her breath, anticipating a response to the brief kiss, but again there was nothing. No spark. No flame. Nothing.

'You look wonderful, darling,' she heard David say, and it was only with a conscious effort that she kept the smile on her face.

'Thank you,' she managed, relieved that the waiter chose that moment to return to their table.

'Are you sure you can't meet me later?' David asked after the waiter had left. 'I thought we could have a cozy little dinner for two.' He reached across the table to take her hand. As he raised it to his lips, his voice lowered seductively. 'And afterward we could go back to my place where I can show you just how much I've missed you.' He turned her hand over.

'David, don't,' April said, pulling her hand free and wondering at the sense of distaste that feathered across her skin.

'What is it, April?' The words came out on a sigh. 'I really don't understand your reluctance, darling, especially when we're going to be married. When two people are in love — '

'But that's just it,' April cut in. 'I'm not sure — ' She broke off, realizing exactly what her words implied.

'You're not sure about what?' David asked, a hint of impatience in his tone now.

April held her annoyance in check, but she could no longer restrain the doubts that had been in her heart all along, waiting to be voiced. 'I'm not sure what my feelings for you really are,' she said truthfully and watched as surprise registered on his handsome features. 'I like you, David,' she went on, wanting to make him understand. 'I thought I loved you, but I'm not sure . . . I'd always thought that when you loved someone there would be no doubts, no questions, only certainty.'

'I see,' David said. 'All you need is a little time. I can wait. I know I haven't always been patient, but that's because I love you.'

April closed her eyes, knowing in her heart of hearts that all the time in the world would not change the way she felt about him.

'Mr. Thornton?' The waiter's voice interrupted her thoughts. 'There's a telephone call for you, sir. You can take it at the bar.'

'Excuse me, darling. I'll be right back.' David followed the waiter, leaving April alone with her thoughts once more. She knew now without a shadow of doubt that she didn't love David. With this realization came a profound sense of relief. She'd been fighting her instincts all along, and now she understood that her reluctance to set a wedding date had stemmed from a subconscious feeling that she was making a mistake.

And it was Quinn she had to thank, for his presence had awakened her heart, and aroused in her emotions and sensations she had never felt before. But more importantly, he had shown her how caring and compassionate, warm and sensitive a man could be.

'I'm sorry, April.' David's voice broke into her reverie. 'I have to go. A man called the office five minutes ago to say he saw Quinn Quartermain wandering around the Seattle Center. He says Quartermain is sporting a beard and mustache. Can you believe it? Normally I'd be inclined to ignore this tip, but the caller happens to be an off-duty policeman and, more to the point, the latest rumor out of L.A. is that Quartermain has skipped town.'

April's heart sank at David's words.

Dear God! Quinn had been spotted! And if someone had recognized him, then it wouldn't be long before other reporters and television crews would be sent out to track him down. Where was he now? she wondered. Did he even know he'd been spotted?

David was beckoning to the waiter. 'I still think he was responsible for that accident.'

'What makes you say that?' April asked, trying to keep the anger from her voice.

'Because he's refused to talk to the press. His reluctance to be questioned and now his disappearing act are sure signs of guilt. And if he is here in Seattle, he's hardly showing regret or remorse for what happened, is he?'

April was too angry to reply.

'Look, darling. I'm sorry about lunch. I'll make it up to you. And don't worry, every bride-to-be has second thoughts. These things have a way of working out. I've got to run. The editor wants a small piece on Quartermain for tonight's paper, regardless of whether or not we find him. Wish me luck,' David said and bent to cover her mouth with his. The kiss was rough and demanding, with none of the tenderness, none of the sweet delicious thrill of longing that seemed to enslave her the moment Quinn's mouth touched hers.

She had no appetite for the food the waiter placed before her and found herself wondering how she could ever have thought herself in love with David. By brushing aside her doubts, David had succeeded only in confirming them. She knew now that she could never marry him.

April had little time over the next few hours to think of anything other than Teresa Santini. It took all of April's tact and diplomacy to appease the near-panicked bride-to-be and convince her that the minor adjustments to the wedding gown could be completed immediately. All that was needed was an addition of two darts on the back of the dress, an adjustment to the hem and a second layer of lace for the headdress.

It was after five by the time April completed the alterations. Teresa had hovered over her throughout the entire procedure and it was not without difficulty that April had managed to control her temper. But the ache in her shoulders was forgotten when Teresa emerged from the fitting room. Exquisite, April thought with a mixture of pride and satisfaction, studying the beautiful creation that she had so lovingly designed and sewn.

To April's intense relief, Teresa could find no fault with the dress. Joyfully she hugged April and Bobbi and after making arrangements to pick up the gown the next day, she bade them good-night.

'You go home. I'll lock up,' April offered after Teresa had left.

'Would you?' Bobbi sounded relieved. 'I'm supposed to be meeting Matt in five minutes.'

'Go!' April ordered, giving her friend a hug.

April locked the door behind Bobbi and let out a sigh. Where was Quinn? she wondered. It was almost six o'clock. Had David tracked him down? She dared not think about it. She returned to her office to tidy her desk. Then, reaching for her jacket, she heard the sound of thunder rumbling in the distance. Back in the outer room, another noise — the sound of someone tapping at the door — caught her attention. She hurried to open it.

'Hello.' Quinn greeted her with a grin, shaking the rain from his hair. 'Nice weather for ducks,' he added as he slipped inside.

Relief washed over April at the sight of him and she felt her heart leap in response to his smile. When he accidentally brushed against her in passing, she felt warmth spread through her as every cell tingled to life.

'Well! Did you manage to soothe the nervous bride?' he asked, glancing around the spacious room.

'Of course!' she told him, unaccountably pleased that he'd asked. 'I just hope the wedding supper is a salad,' she added. 'Otherwise there might be a few seams popping.'

The rich sound of his laughter suddenly filled the air and seconds later she was laughing, too. She would remember this moment forever, she told herself. Happiness enveloped her, leaving her breathless.

It was all Quinn could do not to reach out and touch her. She hadn't been far from his thoughts all afternoon and now seeing her smile, hearing her laugh had quickly erased the feeling of emptiness he'd known as he wandered the streets of Seattle.

No one had followed him. No one had been dogging his footsteps. But instead of feeling relieved, Quinn found he was filled with unease. He'd walked for hours but he could remember little of where he had been and what he had seen.

His eyes came to rest on April. Suddenly he was overwhelmed by the feeling that he'd come home. In that moment the truth was revealed to him. It wasn't enough that his life was in an uproar he thought, acknowledging the emotion. He had to go and fall in love with a woman whose heart belonged to another man, a woman who could never be his.

9

April glanced at Quinn and in the dim light of the car her expression softened into a smile. He'd been asleep for more than an hour but she'd made no move to wake him. She turned her attention back to the road and listened to the gentle swish of the windshield wipers. Though she was beginning to feel cramped and more than a little hungry, the past hour and a half had gone quickly.

At his request she'd given Quinn a quick tour of the boutique. When he'd commented favorably on the layout of the dressing rooms and smiled his approval of the large area they used as a sewing room, she'd barely managed to hide her pleasure.

She'd made no mention of the fact that someone had spotted him at the Seattle Center, feeling he had enough to contend with. And in a short time they would be back in Birch Bay, an unlikely place for anyone to start looking for him.

It was strange, April thought, as she felt Quinn stir beside her, that his sudden reappearance in her life would prove to be as timely as his arrival in the basement garage of that hotel ten years ago.

Quinn woke with a start. It was still raining, but it was little more than a drizzle now, he saw. His neck ached and as he shifted uncomfortably in the seat, he scanned the roadway but recognized nothing.

'Bellingham is up ahead,' April said. 'We could stop and have something to eat if you're hungry.'

'Now that you mention it, I'm starving. How about you?'

'I wouldn't say no,' she said. 'There's a nice restaurant in Fairhaven — that's in the old part of Bellingham.'

'You're the driver,' he said and settled back in the seat.

By the time they reached the

restaurant the rain had stopped completely. The hostess quickly tossed aside the newspaper she'd been reading and smiled a greeting before showing them to a table. As April took her seat she realized she'd forgotten how the dim lighting and the candles flickering on each table gave a certain romantic ambience to the room.

'What would you recommend?' Quinn asked, glancing up from the leather-bound menu.

'If you like prime rib, they serve a king-size cut that hardly leaves room on the plate for anything else.'

'That sounds tempting. I think I'll try it.' Quinn closed the menu and leaned back in his chair, letting his glance slide over her.

Ten years ago he'd glimpsed the promise of beauty in her youthful face, but he had to admit now that she'd surpassed his expectations. Though she'd attempted to confine her rich, dark hair in an elegant knot, it still had a wild, untamed look. And her eyes held a hint of mystery, a lazy sensuality she was totally unaware of. Her nose was small and straight and her lips . . . He stopped; he remembered all too clearly their taste, their texture.

His breath caught in his throat at the sudden overwhelming need that assailed him. His fingers curled convulsively into tight fists, causing a shaft of pain to travel up his injured arm. With great deliberation he released the air that was trapped in his lungs, wondering anew at the depth and strength of his feelings for her. He wanted to touch her, to see her smile and to hear the sound of her laughter. Nothing had ever felt so right.

'I'll have the smaller cut,' April said. 'That way I might have room for dessert. They serve a scrumptious mud pie here,' she added.

The food was delectable, and throughout the meal their conversation was relaxed and friendly. Quinn asked questions about her childhood, and made her laugh with tales of the pranks he and Ian had played on each other in school. He was attentive and amusing and April found herself wishing the night would never end.

By the time the waiter brought the check, they were both surprised to note that it was past eleven. While Quinn took care of things, April stood in the shadows of the foyer. As she waited, her glance fell on the hostess's discarded newspaper.

Suddenly a headline on the corner of the page caught her eye: 'Update on Movie Star Sasha Gray's Death — Man Sought.'

With trembling fingers April reached for the paper and began to read:

This morning the Los Angeles Police Department released their report on the accident that claimed the life of rising young star Sasha Gray. In a surprising development they are asking for help in locating a man seen leaving the scene of the accident.

'Shall we go?' Quinn asked, turning to her.

'Wait — look at this!' She pointed to the headline.

He almost snatched the paper from her hands as he, too, read the headline. His heart started to pound in his chest and his breathing became labored as the words on the paper registered in his brain.

'I've got to call Ian. Do you know what this means?' His voice was choked with emotion as he met her gaze. 'Thank God! It means I'm not going insane.'

April had no time to react as Quinn pulled her into his arms and held her tightly against him. Joy for him splintered through her and she felt hot tears sting her eyes. Through the haze she saw that the hostess was watching them with interest.

Quinn released her, then held her at arm's length. The sight of the tears shimmering in her eyes brought an expression of love and tenderness to his face.

Glancing over Quinn's shoulder, April could see that the hostess was still staring at them. 'Why don't you wait and call Ian from the cabin?' she suggested, casually motioning toward the woman. Seconds later they were outside, crossing the street to the car.

'Thanks,' Quinn said as he struggled with the seat belt. 'Another few minutes and she might have recognized me. Now she'll never be sure.'

'Ian's probably been calling all day. He'll be frantic wondering where we've been,' April said when they were once more underway. 'I'm surprised he didn't call the boutique, but then again he had no reason to.'

'Right,' Quinn agreed. 'Could you turn on the interior light? I want to read the report again.'

April obliged, and as she drove the remaining miles to the cabin she could almost feel the anticipation, the excitement in the man next to her. For herself she was caught between happiness and sorrow — happiness at the possibility of

Quinn's discovering the truth of that fateful night, but sadness at the realization that his time with them was running out.

'It says here the police have some more questions they want to ask me,' Quinn said, breaking into her thoughts. 'I hope Robson put them in touch with Ian,' he added as April pulled into the driveway.

But April wasn't listening. Her attention was focused on the cabin. 'That's funny,' she said, switching off the engine.

'What?'

'All the lights are on,' she murmured, opening the driver's door and stepping out.

'Did you leave them on?'

'Only the one above the front door,' she told him.

Quinn moved quickly to bar her way and the serious expression on his face alarmed her.

'Get back inside the car,' he ordered, in a tone she'd never heard him use before. But when Quinn turned and cautiously made his way around the corner of the cabin, she was right behind him.

Light spilled across the patio from the kitchen and living-room windows. April gasped in shock when she saw the door of the cabin standing open.

'Dammit, April, I told you to get back in the car!' Quinn's tone was angry. He gripped her shoulder. 'Stay here,' he told her, but again she ignored him as he hurried inside.

'Oh God!' The words were wrenched from her when she saw the upheaval before her. Newspapers, magazines and the cushions from the couch and chair were strewn all over the floor. In the kitchen, pots, pans and a number of cutlery items lay everywhere.

Quinn glanced around and anger burned through him. His initial impression was one of total chaos, but on closer examination, he could see that the intruder had been bent on disorder rather than destruction.

His gaze flew to April and at the shocked expression on her face he cursed under his breath. He should have been annoyed with her for ignoring his order to stay outside, but as he gathered her in his arms his anger quickly evaporated. He'd simply wanted to protect her, fearful that the intruder might still be in the cabin. The silence echoing around them, however, was reminiscent of a tomb.

'Who could have done this?' she asked softly. Then her heart stopped as a thought surfaced. 'It was him . . . that man.' She drew away to look at Quinn and she could see that the same thought had occurred to him. 'I don't understand. What does he want?' April tried to keep her voice even, but Quinn heard the hint of fear and the touch of desperation in her tone.

He had no answer. Drawing her close, he tightened his hold and gave himself up to the overpowering need to cherish, protect and love.

April felt the fear and tension slowly

melt away. Never before had simply being held in someone's arms made her feel so cared for. What she found most puzzling was that each time she was in his arms the intense feeling of belonging grew stronger.

After several long minutes, Quinn loosened his hold and eased away from April. Although he was sure the intruder had gone, for his own peace of mind he wanted to check out the bedrooms.

'Would you please stay here while I check the rest of the house?' he asked quietly.

April nodded and even managed a smile. Quinn gently brushed her cheek with his hand, then made his way down the hall.

His was the only bedroom that appeared to have been touched. His suitcase lay on the floor and his clothes had been tossed around the room, but nothing was missing. After tidying up a little, he returned to the living room.

April looked up. 'How bad is it?' she

asked, continuing to pick up the scattered newspapers.

'My room seems to be the only one disturbed. And even then it's not much. He must have tired of the game,' said Quinn. He bent to pick up a chair cushion.

'Nothing seems to be missing here,' April said as she folded a magazine. 'Actually, it looks worse than it really is,' she added.

They were both silent for a while as they worked steadily to clean up. Lifting a magazine, April found the telephone. The receiver was on the floor beside it. 'What about Ian? Are you still going to call him?' she asked.

'It's well past midnight,' Quinn said. 'I wouldn't want to wake the children.' He put the telephone on the end table. 'My guess is that the man responsible for this must have arrived shortly after we left this morning. When he realized we had gone, he broke in and vented his annoyance by throwing things around. I bet Ian's been getting a busy signal all day and probably thinks your phone is out of order.'

April nodded. Quinn's explanation seemed logical. She stood up, stretching her cramped legs. The living room was almost back to normal now, so she moved to the kitchen and began gathering the scattered utensils.

Quinn picked up the remaining cushion and set it back in place. Turning, he noticed a rainbow-colored chiffon scarf lying on the floor. Frowning, he bent to retrieve it. As his fingers touched the delicate material a succession of images, all of them of Sasha, suddenly appeared before him. A dizzying sensation enveloped him, causing beads of perspiration to break out on his forehead. For a moment he thought he might pass out.

He sank to his knees, feeling as though his body had sustained a devastating blow. It took every ounce of strength he possessed to reach out and pick up the scarf.

'Sasha!' The name came out in an anguished groan as he crushed the fabric in his hand.

At the sound of the heart-wrenching moan April spun around. Racing into the living room, she saw Quinn kneeling on the floor, clutching a piece of material in his hand.

Something was wrong; she could feel it in the air. Without another thought she hurried to his side. The touch of her fingers on his shoulder brought his head up. April almost gasped aloud at the anguish in his eyes.

'Quinn! What is it? What happened?' She knelt down beside him, feeling totally helpless.

It took Quinn several seconds to answer. 'This scarf . . . it was Sasha's,' he said at last, holding it out to her.

'Are you sure?' April asked gently. The scarf had obviously triggered his memory. Perhaps this would be the breakthrough he'd been waiting for, April thought with a surge of hope. 'Tell me about it,' she coaxed quietly, all the while praying she was doing the right thing.

Quinn closed his eyes and inhaled deeply. His initial shock at finding the scarf was over, and his control was slowly returning. He tried to relax, fighting the tension within him, wanting desperately not to lose the pictures that were taking shape in his mind. He breathed out, keeping his eyes closed, afraid that once he opened them the memory would evaporate like steam from a cup of coffee.

'It was a prop from the movie. Sasha liked it so much that when we finished filming, she asked if she could keep it as a memento.'

'And she was wearing it on the night of the accident?' April prodded.

'Yes!' Quinn's voice was little more than a whisper. As they'd made their way across the parking lot to his car, Sasha had stopped for a moment to tie the scarf around her hair, a rather futile action, he'd thought, unlocking the passenger door.

As she approached the car, he noticed her glance slide past him, over his shoulder. Her expression changed instantly to alarm, but before he could make a move, something hard and solid had come down on his head, dropping him into a black void.

Of course! He'd been knocked out! That explained why he hadn't been able to remember! But his euphoria at this revelation was short-lived . . . The accident had happened two hours later on the other side of town! He'd been found sprawled half in and half out of the driver's side. Sasha's lifeless body had been in the passenger seat beside him. How had they got there?

Quinn groaned in renewed frustration; he was still no nearer to solving the mystery. Once again only a small piece of the puzzle had been revealed, leaving him dangling in midair like a parachutist caught in a tree.

April's heart ached for him. Her hand reached out and lightly caressed his bent head. As her fingers stroked the springy softness of his hair she felt her pulse quicken.

He seemed deep in thought, completely unaware of her presence. She felt sure he must be thinking of Sasha. Slowly his head came up and she found herself staring into eyes that were misty with sorrow. Her arms went around him. Drawing him toward her she gave in to the need to comfort.

They knelt together, one human being consoling another. But as if the wind had shifted, the atmosphere suddenly changed and became charged with electricity. Awareness crackled between them like a bolt of lightning flashing across the sky.

Wherever his body touched hers, April felt as though her skin were on fire. The heat of passion coursed through her veins with a ferocity she'd never known before.

With his left hand Quinn found the pins and released April's hair from its chignon. His fingers threaded through the silky tresses and he felt his body tremble with need. He drew away to look into eyes that were vividly green and alight with a hunger that almost matched his own.

April watched Quinn's face inch closer. Her eyelids floated down and her mouth opened on a sigh as Quinn's lips met hers.

She'd expected passion, hot and turbulent. Instead, his lips were as gentle as the summer rain as he planted tiny, tantalizing kisses on her mouth.

She whimpered in frustration. By way of answer to her incoherent pleading, Quinn's kisses became more urgent, demanding a response she was eager to give.

Little explosions of light and sensation raced along her nerve endings, taking erotic messages to every cell and awakening needs she'd only dreamed of.

So this was desire, this exciting, breathtaking hunger that was driving her higher and higher, closer and closer to the edge of reason!

Desire was spiraling through Quinn, too, with the speed and force of a tornado. Her lips tasted of some heavenly nectar; his tongue dipped into her mouth and he wanted nothing more than to lose himself in the joy that was April.

He'd never known a feeling like this or a power so strong. Her quiet sensuality, her compassionate nature, her ability to give without thought for herself had captured his heart. This was the woman he'd been searching for all his life. Here was his soul mate, his one true love.

April felt as if she were floating on a cloud of pure sensation. So this was passion! Never before had she felt so alive, so aware of her own femininity. For the first time in her life her body ached for fulfillment as Quinn silently promised her the moon.

Had he kissed Sasha this way? The question came from some dark corner of her mind to slash through her euphoria and send her plummeting back to earth.

He'd been talking of Sasha, thinking about the woman he had loved and lost so tragically. Could it be that as a result of his pain and grief he was imagining that she was Sasha?

With a moan of despair she broke the kiss and struggled to her feet. A searing pain tore at her heart and she fought to control breathing that was decidedly ragged, a body that was trembling with need.

Not for anything did she want Quinn to see how deeply he'd affected her. With a poise and dignity she hadn't known she possessed, she straightened her shoulders and turned to see Quinn slowly rising. Clinging to the last vestiges of her control she met his gaze, only to see a look of guilt and sadness on his face.

April blinked furiously, trying to combat the sudden sting of tears that threatened to blind her. She wanted to run to the sanctuary of her room, bury her face in her pillow and weep until all the pain inside her was gone, but she couldn't move.

Turning away, Quinn's glance dropped to the chiffon scarf that he still clutched in his hand. A question darted across his mind. Where had it come from? How had the scarf come to be in the cabin? The answer was all too obvious — the intruder had to have dropped it! What other explanation could there be? And in that moment Quinn realized that the intruder and the man in the newspaper report — the man the police wanted to question — were one and the same.

Alarm flickered through him as he swung back to April. For reasons Quinn had yet to determine, he was being stalked. Good God! His glance swept over April. If anything should happen to her! An icy hand clutched at his heart, robbing him of breath. In order to ensure April's safety, he would have to leave. He exhaled slowly. But not yet, not tonight.

His eyes came to rest once more on her face. She looked utterly defenseless and totally bewitching and he longed to pull her back into his arms. But if he did, he knew he'd never be able to let her go.

'I think I'll leave the rest of the cleaning up till the morning,' April said, her voice not quite steady. She didn't wait for an answer. She'd seen all she needed to see.

April leaned heavily against the door of her bedroom and stood in the darkness, letting the night soothe her battered heart. She undressed slowly as a cavalcade of thoughts and impressions filed across her mind.

Not till she was lying in bed could she bring herself to face what she had been sidestepping from the moment Quinn had arrived on her doorstep less than a week ago.

She was in love with him! What other explanation could there be for the intensity of her feelings? Only when she was with him did she feel completely alive; it was as though he were an integral part of her that had been missing.

April let her thoughts drift along this path of discovery, realizing now with sudden insight that she had fallen in love with Quinn one balmy night in June ten years ago.

Though she'd only been sixteen, those first stirrings of love, like a forgotten seedling, had quietly taken root, lying dormant over the years waiting for his return. But a fairy-tale ending was not in the cards, April thought. Tears began to trickle down her face and onto her pillow.

April had not expected to sleep at all, and when she awoke it was something of a surprise when she saw that it was nearly ten o'clock.

Throwing back the covers, she pulled on her housecoat and slid her feet into her slippers. She could smell coffee and she made her way to the kitchen, her heart quickening in anticipation of seeing Quinn.

Disappointment washed over her when she found the kitchen empty. That Quinn had tidied up was obvious by its spotless condition and she found herself touched anew by his thoughtfulness. Pouring herself a cup of coffee she wondered if he had already talked to Ian. Was he even now preparing to leave?

Pain, sharp and agonizing, stabbed at her heart. Raising the cup to her lips, she sipped the hot liquid and tried unsuccessfully to steer her thoughts away from Quinn.

The sound of a vehicle pulling into the gravel driveway had her heart pounding against her ribs. Could it be the stranger? Fear held her captive and she stood staring at the kitchen window.

When David's familiar figure walked blithely past, April was both astonished and perturbed. He was the last person she'd expected to see and she was in no way prepared for his untimely arrival. With a sinking feeling she set her coffee on the counter and went to answer his knock.

'David! What on earth are you doing here?'

'What kind of a welcome is that?' David asked, eyeing her curiously. 'Aren't you pleased to see me?' His voice held a teasing note.

'Yes, of course,' April replied, feeling rather flustered. 'I'm sorry. Come in.'

'I'm on my way to Vancouver,' he told her. 'The Prince and Princess of Wales are due to arrive at the airport this afternoon on a brief stopover on their way to Japan. I'm also checking out another lead on Quartermain. I didn't manage to track him down yesterday, but after the news story last night we had numerous calls saying he was seen heading for the Canadian border. I'm inclined to disbelieve them. He's probably on his way back to L.A. Anyway, I thought you might like to come with me. We could spend some time together,' he finished with a flourish.

'David, I . . . ' April's voice faltered as she heard a sound from the hall. The sight of Quinn with a towel around his neck and wearing only jeans emptied her mind of every coherent thought and brought a look of panic to her face.

David glanced questioningly over his shoulder, in time to see someone disappear down the hallway.

'Was that Greg? Shouldn't he be in school?' His eyes came to rest on April's pink cheeks, then traveled down to take in her tousled state. 'That wasn't Greg, was it?' His gaze came back to her.

'David, I — '

'Was it?' he repeated.

'No, but you don't understand,' April said, feeling compelled to try to explain.

'Oh, but you're wrong. I understand perfectly,' came the prompt reply. 'In fact, it explains a number of things very clearly.'

April held his gaze, refusing to look away. She could understand his anger, but she had nothing to feel guilty about. He believed the worst of her, she could see it in his face — and while this was not the way she had wanted things to end, there was nothing more to say. Slipping the engagement ring from her finger, she held it out to him.

In the bedroom Quinn was pacing up and down. When he'd emerged from the bathroom and heard voices, his one thought had been that the stranger had returned. He'd reached the hallway in time to hear April call the visitor 'David'. But by then it had been too late.

Since returning to his room, he'd been listening to the muffled sound of their voices, and it had taken all Quinn's self-control not to charge back in and find out what was happening. The brief glimpse he'd had of April's fiancé hadn't exactly enamored him of the man, but then he knew that his feelings for April made for a prejudiced point of view.

At the sound of the front door closing, Quinn went into the living room. He clenched his jaw when he saw April's sad expression, and it was all he could do not to take her in his arms and try to comfort her.

'April?' Her name came out on a

fragile thread of emotion. 'What happened? Are you all right?' he asked. He reached out tentatively to touch her hair.

'Yes. Yes, I'm fine,' she told him, surprised at the look of concern on his face, concern and something more.

'I'm sorry about barging in on you like that. When I heard voices I thought — ' He stopped.

'It's all right, really,' April said, looking down at her ringless hand.

Quinn's glance followed hers. 'He did see me. Damn! I know how it must have looked to him . . . I'll go after him.' It was the least he could do, he thought as he made to leave.

'No! No, that won't be necessary.' That he was willing to go after David warmed her immeasurably. Tears gathered in her eyes and before she could blink them away one escaped, tracing a solitary path down her cheek.

'I don't understand,' she heard Quinn say. 'If I tell him who I am and explain why I'm here — ' His thumb caressed her cheek, wiping away the stray tear.

'Please, there's no need,' April interrupted, wishing with all her heart he would take her in his arms. 'For the past few months I've been having second thoughts about my engagement to David. I'd already decided to break it off. I'm just sorry it happened the way it did.'

April's words, spoken with sincerity and the ring of truth, sent a feeling of joy surging through him. If she wasn't in love with David and the engagement was off, there was no longer any reason for him to hold back. Her response to his kisses told him she wasn't unmoved by him . . . It was a beginning . . .

Quinn abruptly brought his thoughts to a halt. How could he have forgotten about the stranger? While there was nothing he wanted more than to hold April close and tell her he loved her, at this point in time her safety was his primary concern. In order to ensure it he would have to leave . . . now.

10

'April,' Quinn began hesitatingly, 'I have to go back to Los Angeles.'

Bewilderment and pain clouded her eyes as Quinn's words registered. Though this was the moment she'd been dreading, nothing had prepared her for the numbing sadness that overwhelmed her. He was leaving and with him he would be taking her heart.

'I called Ian,' she heard Quinn say. 'After giving me hell, he told me to call the Los Angeles police department, and ask for a Detective Morgan. Said he wanted to talk to me, urgently — '

'And?' April asked evenly, while inside her heart was slowly breaking apart.

'He wants me to look at a mug shot. They believe the man they're looking for, the man who left the scene of the accident is someone called Donald

Grayson. He was recently released from prison and he never checked in with his parole officer. He was serving four years for armed robbery.'

'Armed robbery!' April could hardly believe her ears. 'Do you know this man?'

'No. His name didn't mean a thing. But when Detective Morgan described Grayson to me . . . Well, the description matched the one you gave of the blond, blue-eyed stranger.' He stopped, his expression turning thoughtful. 'And he also told me something else. Grayson was Sasha's ex-husband.'

April stared at Quinn, surprised by his calm acceptance of this startling information. This piece of news certainly shed some light on the puzzle, but obviously it had done nothing to jog Quinn's memory.

'Did you tell the police that we think Grayson is here?' April asked suddenly.

'Yes,' he replied. 'And I also told them about my plan.'

'Plan?'

'I didn't sleep much. I spent the night trying to think of a way to flush this guy out. And after hearing what the detective had to tell me, I'm convinced it's the only way to catch him.'

'Catch him?' April said anxiously, sensing that she wasn't going to like Quinn's plan at all.

'If Grayson is watching the cabin — and I'm pretty sure he is — when he sees me leaving, he'll follow. I'm banking on the fact that he missed us yesterday and this time he won't want to lose me. I plan to drive to the Bellingham airport and if Detective Morgan comes through with his end of the plan, a couple of detectives from the Bellingham sheriff's office will be waiting there for us.' Though his plan was by no means foolproof, his main objective was to draw Grayson away from the cabin — away from April.

'But how can you be sure he'll follow you?'

'I'll just have to make sure,' Quinn said. 'I'm going to make quite a production of my departure — make sure he knows I'm leaving. He'll follow,' he finished with a confidence he was far from feeling. Detective Morgan hadn't thought much of the plan, but hadn't been able to come up with anything more workable.

'But . . . '

'April — ' Quinn's tone was gentle, soothing ' — I appreciate your concern, believe me. But don't you see? I have to do this. Grayson is my only link to finding out what happened that night. I need to confront him.'

'Yes, but — '

His finger briefly touched her lips, effectively silencing her protests and at the same time sending a ripple of longing racing through her. She understood the reason behind his actions, but that didn't mean she approved.

She swallowed. 'And you're leaving now?'

'Yes. As soon as I finish packing. You do understand?' He held her gaze for a moment, wishing he didn't have to leave, wishing there was another way.

'Of course,' she said quickly, and tried to ignore the pain that was squeezing at her heart. She would never see him again! The realization jolted her and as she watched him walk away, she had to bite down on her lower lip to stop herself from crying out.

In her room, she dressed in a pair of jeans and a sweater. When the telephone rang she dropped the hairbrush on the dressing table and hurried to answer it.

'April!' Greg's voice came over the line.

'Greg? Is something wrong?' Her heart started to hammer in her breast.

'No, nothing's wrong. I forgot to tell you that school let out early today. I'm at Mark's. Can you come and pick me up?'

'I'll be there in a few minutes.' April replaced the receiver and turned to find Quinn, suitcase in hand, watching her. Her heart wavered at the sight of him and tears welled in her eyes. She blinked them away. It was all she could do to keep her breathing even as flashes of the special moments they'd shared replayed like broken melodies inside her head. He would be gone when she returned with Greg, she thought woodenly, and suddenly she wanted it to be that way, knowing she wouldn't be able to watch him leave.

'Ah . . . ' She cleared her throat, her voice suddenly thick with emotion. 'That was Greg. I have to pick him up.'

'Oh.' Quinn's gaze lingered over features that were engraved forever on his mind. 'Tell him I said goodbye. And tell him that when all this is over, I'll be back.' He set the suitcase on the floor and came to a halt in front of her. 'I *will* be back, April.' Quinn's hand came up to touch her hair. 'There's so much I want to say . . . '

April felt her knees go weak as her body drifted towards his. The husky timbre of his voice was infinitely seductive.

'I don't know how I can ever thank

you.' His words were like knives being driven into her heart. She didn't want his gratitude — she wanted his love.

Calling on every iota of strength, she drew away. 'I've got to go,' she said, surprised that her voice sounded normal. 'Good luck!' Picking up her keys and purse from the table where she'd dropped them the evening before, she turned and ran.

Quinn stood rooted to the spot. Every instinct was shouting at him to call her back, to gather her in his arms and tell her he wasn't going anywhere without her. 'Damn!' The oath reverberated off the walls and he drew a hand through his hair.

He glanced around at the now-familiar surroundings. He was already beginning to miss its warmth, its loving atmosphere and he knew that the sense of family, the peacefulness and contentment he'd known here were everything that had been missing from his life. But without April, the house was simply a wooden building, four walls and a roof.

With a sigh that echoed from the depths of his heart, he bent to pick up his suitcase.

Suddenly the sound of footsteps captured his attention. April must have forgotten something. Crossing the room, he opened the door — to find himself staring into the barrel of a hand gun.

Quinn lifted his gaze and met a pair of cold blue eyes.

'You!' Involuntarily he took a step back as recognition and remembrance flowed through him, flooding his mind and swamping his senses. This was Grayson, Sasha's ex-husband, and the man responsible for her death.

The events of that night, which till now had been locked in some dark corner of his mind, tumbled forth like rocks down a mountainside.

'It was you! You were the one driving the car, not me,' Quinn said, recalling now how he'd emerged from a state of unconsciousness, his head pounding, to find himself huddled on the floor in the

254

back seat of his car.

Slowly he'd eased himself onto the seat, the sound of his movements muffled by Sasha's sobs. Dazed and disoriented, he'd found himself staring into the rearview mirror at the cold blue eyes of the man who stood before him now. Seconds later had come the squeal of tires and the sound of Sasha screaming his name.

'It's too bad you got such a good look at me,' Grayson said in a voice that sent a shiver of unease down Quinn's spine.

'I'm not the only one who knows you were there,' Quinn said, his eyes alert, already looking for an opportunity to disarm Grayson. 'The police are looking for you. Take my advice and turn yourself in.'

Grayson's harsh laughter filled the cabin. 'Turn myself in! You must be crazy! I'm not going back to that stinking jail.'

'I wouldn't bet on it,' Quinn challenged him.

'You're the only one who knows I was driving, the only one who can identify me. When I dragged you from that wreck and put you by the driver's door, I thought you were dead. I should have made sure, but there wasn't time.'

'What do you plan to do now?' Quinn asked.

'I plan to take care of unfinished business — and this time I don't intend to leave any witnesses.' Grayson motioned with the gun toward the open door. 'Let's go. We're gonna take a drive down the coast.'

Though the implication was obvious, Quinn had little concern for himself. His thoughts were on April and Greg. He felt sure they would be back any minute and their safety was uppermost in his mind. Silently he sent up a prayer that he and Grayson would be gone before they returned.

★ ★ ★

'Looks like we have company,' Greg said as April came to a halt at the stop sign that was situated a short distance from the cabin.

'Company?' April, who'd been silent and preoccupied throughout the short drive home, cast a glance towards the cabin, noticing the truck parked by the garage. Her heart stopped at the sight of two men who suddenly appeared on the patio. One she instantly recognized as Quinn. But the other? It had to be Grayson. And what was in his hand? Was it a gun?

April's heart began to pound. Dear God! Quinn's plan had gone haywire. What could she do?

With a calmness she was far from feeling April drove past the cabin and turned into the driveway beyond. Time was of the essence.

'Hey, sis! What are you doing? You missed the turn,' Greg said as he turned to his sister.

'Greg. Listen to me.' April's tone was serious. 'I want you to run to the phone booth at the end of the street and call the police. Tell them to get here as fast as they can.'

'Why?' Greg asked, bewildered.

'That man we just saw with Quinn . . . I'm not sure, but I think he has a gun,' April answered. 'I'll explain everything later. Just do as I ask.'

'What are *you* going to do?' Greg asked as he reached for the door handle.

'I don't know. Try to stall them until the police get here, I guess. Hurry!'

Without looking at Greg, April opened the car door and quickly made her way toward the garage. All she could think about was Quinn. If anything happened to him . . . She rounded the corner — and came face to face with the object of her thoughts.

'April!' Her name was torn from his throat as his worst fear was suddenly realized. 'Run! Get out of here!' he urged, a mere second before Grayson landed a glancing blow, sending him to his knees.

'Stay where you are!' Grayson ordered.

But April had no intention of running anywhere. Instead she knelt beside Quinn. 'Are you all right?'

'Yes,' he said quietly, fighting the anger, the despair, that were threatening to overwhelm him, wishing with all his heart he had never come here, yet knowing as he held her gaze that his life had changed irrevocably because he had.

Quinn gently touched April's cheek in a gesture of comfort. God, how he loved her! Surely there had to be a way to disable Grayson! Quinn turned, hoping to catch Grayson off guard, but already he'd taken a step back out of reach and the gun in his hand was pointed squarely at Quinn's chest.

Suddenly a movement at the corner of the cabin caught Quinn's eye. He felt April tense beside him and knew she too had noticed the figure. It was Greg! And in his hand he held what looked to be a broken oar.

Quinn abruptly brought his attention back to Grayson. He had to distract him, had to keep talking in order to cover the sound of Greg's approach.

'Please! Leave her out of this. It's me you want,' Quinn said as he pulled April into his arms.

Grayson's smile was ugly. 'You must think I'm really stupid,' came the reply. 'She comes too. Now, let's get out of here. I've wasted enough time already,' he added, motioning them both toward the truck.

Quinn attempted to get to his feet, then pretended to stumble, noting as he did that Grayson's grip on the gun had relaxed.

Now! Quinn silently screamed at Greg who was only a few feet away. Hit him now!

The blow when it came was totally unexpected, stunning Grayson and effectively knocking the gun from his grasp. Quinn jumped to his feet and in his haste to reach Grayson almost knocked April to the ground. Within moments he was bending over their captor, landing a resounding left hook that sent Grayson sprawling once more, this time unconscious.

'We got him! We got him!' Greg's ecstatic cries and grinning features told their own story.

Quinn's face broke into a wide smile but he remained poised over Grayson's inert form.

Dazed and confused April took in the scene. Everything had happened so quickly, but now in the aftermath she realized how Greg's reckless action could well have ended in disaster.

'Greg . . . ' April had difficulty getting out the words. 'I told you to get the police. Dear God! He had a gun! You could have been killed!' She shivered at the thought that the outcome could well have been horribly different.

Greg was instantly at her side. 'Sis, I didn't see the gun. Listen, I'm sorry. I was just trying to help. I thought if I went to call the police they would take forever to get here. So I grabbed the first thing I could find and came around the other side of the cabin. He didn't hear a thing. Boy! It was like something right out of one of your movies.' Greg brandished the broken oar and flashed a triumphant look at Quinn.

'Greg . . . ' April was at a loss for words once more.

'Don't be angry with him, April,' Quinn intervened. 'If you want to blame someone, then all this is my fault.'

Grayson groaned and Quinn turned his attention back to the man on the ground. 'I think maybe we'd better call the police.'

While they waited for Sheriff Jeffries to arrive, Quinn, with Greg's help, brought Grayson into the cabin, where they immobilized him completely by tying him up.

As a means of working out her own anxiety April busied herself in the kitchen making tea, all the while listening as Quinn tried to answer Greg's questions.

'And you didn't remember a thing about the accident?' asked Greg in fascination.

'That's right,' Quinn said patiently. 'I was convinced I had amnesia — and it wasn't until last night that I realized what had really happened. It wasn't amnesia — I'd simply been knocked out. Grayson must have seen Sasha on that late-night talk show,' he explained. 'My guess is he came down to the studio and waited for her in the parking lot. He probably expected her to be alone. After knocking me out he bundled me into the back of the car. I must have been out for a couple of hours — and only regained consciousness shortly before the crash. Long enough to get a good look at Grayson at the wheel, but I guess the trauma of the accident wiped it temporarily from my mind.'

'Ian said they found me lying half in and half out of the driver's side of the car,' Quinn went on, 'and so I simply assumed I'd been driving. But subconsciously I couldn't shake the feeling that something was out of whack.'

'It's nice to know that your instincts were right,' April said with a smile.

The sound of a siren suddenly filled the air, heralding the arrival of the police. Sheriff Karl Jeffries was a heavyset man in his late forties with graying hair and a friendly smile. When Quinn introduced himself and explained what had happened the sheriff took everything in stride. 'Detective Morgan from the L.A.P.D. called this morning and told us of your plan, Mr. Quartermain. In fact, I'd just dispatched a car to the airport when your call came in,' he told them.

Glancing at Grayson as one of the officers led the prisoner outside, the sheriff's tone became serious. 'I don't have to tell you that you were very lucky. Anyway, I'm going to have to ask you all to come down to the station and make a statement.'

'Of course,' Quinn replied. 'And I'm sure the L.A.P.D. will be only too happy to hear what I have to say. I hope they throw the book at him this time.'

April was silent during the short ride to the police station. She and Greg sat in the back seat of the sheriff's car while Quinn sat up front. Once at the station, Quinn disappeared into the sheriff's office.

Twenty minutes later April signed the statement the officer had typed. When she emerged from the small room where she'd been asked to wait, she noticed that the noise level in the station had risen considerably. The reason was soon apparent; she saw Quinn and Greg standing at the front desk surrounded by a veritable bevy of reporters and cameramen. That Quinn's identity had been discovered was obvious, and despite the sorrow she felt returning, she found herself admiring the calm, no-nonsense way he handled the barrage of questions.

Greg, of course, was reveling in the

attention and April hung back, reluctant to drag him away from his moment of glory.

'Mr. Quartermain!' The sheriff's loud voice cut through the noise and with a few words of apology, Quinn withdrew. It wasn't long before April was able to round up Greg and locate the driver who'd been assigned to take them home.

It was almost dusk when the police car turned into the driveway. Greg instantly asked if he could bike over to Mark's, and April consented, knowing he was eager to tell his friend all about the excitement of having helped capture a criminal. He would also enjoy the thrill of divulging the identity of their house-guest!

After Greg had gone, April wandered restlessly around the cabin, thinking back on the past few days and all that had happened. Quinn's suitcase stood in the living room, a painful reminder that he would soon be walking out of her life forever.

The telephone rang, shattering the stillness and she jumped. The caller was a reporter, the first of many. How they had acquired the phone number she had no idea. After the eighth call in a span of a little over five minutes she slammed the receiver back in place and gently massaged her aching head. When the phone rang yet again she pulled on a jacket and slipped outside.

Anger rippled through her at the thought of the last caller's offer. Would she be interested in giving an exclusive interview, in which she would recount her days with Quinn Quartermain, famous celebrity? She would, of course, be paid extremely well. Disgusted and dismayed, April had firmly declined.

She found it painful enough to face the fact that Quinn would be returning to L.A. He had no reason to stay. She was already beginning to miss him and found herself wondering if this incredible feeling of loneliness that was descending on her would stay with her forever. All she would have would be the memories of the minutes and hours they had spent together. She loved him, totally, completely and without reservation — an everlasting kind of love as precious to her as life itself.

April settled in the old rocking chair, letting the slowly descending darkness cradle her in its soothing embrace. Her life would never be the same, yet there was a sense of joy in the knowledge that she was capable of such a depth of emotion.

The crunch of a car's tires on the gravel outside alerted her instantly. April's heart tripped over itself in anticipation, and when Quinn appeared it was all she could do not to jump up and run to him.

The November night air was bracing, filled with the promise of snow soon to come, but Quinn hardly noticed the chill as his eyes took in April sitting in the old rocking chair. He walked toward her, wanting to take her in his arms and kiss her until kisses weren't enough, touch her until she was quivering with desire.

But for the second time in as many hours, fear held him prisoner. Not the kind of fear he'd experienced earlier when their lives had been in danger — though he never wanted to live through a nightmare like that again — but a fear that left him feeling infinitely more vulnerable. The fear that he might be mistaken in his belief that she cared for him. He couldn't be wrong! The cry came from his heart.

'Waiting for me?' Quinn asked softly, restraining with some difficulty the growing need to pull her into his arms. With a control that had his insides trembling, he smiled and offered his hand. Gently he pulled her to her feet.

His smile was her undoing. Her heart began to skip crazily in her breast and for the life of her she could neither quell the surge of longing that swept through her nor bank the look of love in her eyes.

Ever watchful, Quinn saw her reaction and in that moment the fear that had held him in its grip dissolved as quickly as a snowflake melting in the sun. His throat tightened with emotion. He had nothing to lose and everything to gain.

'April.' Quinn's voice was low and husky and filled with raw emotion. She couldn't speak, was even afraid to breathe in case she broke the fragile spell that was weaving its magic around her. His hand moved to capture her jaw and his thumb gently, erotically caressed her lips. 'I love you,' he said, laying his heart at her feet.

As he watched, her eyes instantly filled with tears, making them look like bright, iridescent jewels. And in their shining depths he saw a look of such love and tenderness that it stole his breath away.

April thought her heart would explode. The words, spoken with total sincerity brought a joy so exquisite that she wanted to cry out. Dear God! To have this man love her. Was it possible? Could dreams come true?

Her hand trembled as she raised it to touch his cheek in a gesture that spoke volumes.

Quinn captured her hand and brought it to his lips, then with infinite tenderness he drew her into his arms, lowering his mouth to meet hers in a kiss that sealed their fate. Slowly, inevitably their bodies came together until neither of them was aware of anything else but the other.

April thought that the kiss was like being taken on a magical journey. She floated in an airless, timeless vacuum, where her only contact with the world was Quinn, his lips, and the sweet pulse of desire she could feel coursing through her. She couldn't get close enough, nor could she quench the overwhelming thirst she had for him . . . all of him.

She moaned in protest when his mouth left hers but when her eyes fluttered open, she sighed with relief, for he was only a breath away.

'I'm not sure I believe this is

happening,' April said as she gazed up at him.

'Believe it.' Quinn smiled at her.

'I thought . . . I mean . . . I know you had feelings for Sasha . . . ' she said. Her words trailed away.

Surprise registered on his face. 'Are you saying you thought I was in love with Sasha?'

April nodded.

'I liked her, yes, but we were friends, nothing more. I love you.'

The sincerity in his voice was unmistakable and at his words, her heart soared.

'April, my love,' he drew her against his chest, 'I need to hear you say it.' Quinn's voice wavered fractionally, revealing the depth of his vulnerability.

'I love you. I think I always have,' April confessed.

Quinn's mouth found hers once more, transporting them both to a world where only they existed. Higher and higher they flew as Quinn unlocked the secrets of her soul. She was all woman, giving unconditionally, loving him with a capacity that knew no bounds. But much as he loved her, much as he needed her, now was not the time to make that ultimate journey of discovery. He wanted to savor the moment of her sweet surrender and share with her his own gift of love.

He broke the kiss and buried his face in the scented swirl of her hair. He held her tightly against him, waiting for his heartbeat to slow, waiting for his control to return.

He drew away. 'Marry me!' The words were more of an order than a request and April looked at him with shining eyes.

'I thought you'd never ask,' she said, all the while aware of her runaway heartbeat.

'Tonight?' he asked, wishing it were possible, afraid the happiness enveloping him might disappear.

April considered his suggestion. 'That really doesn't give me enough time,' she said thoughtfully.

'For what?' he asked, his brow wrinkling in a frown.

'To make my wedding dress,' she told him.

'Ah! Your wedding dress,' Quinn said. An image of April wearing a beautiful bridal gown, walking down the aisle toward him, floated into his mind. 'How much time do you need?' he asked, dropping a kiss on her nose.

'Well, I wouldn't want to rush a project as special as this one. I might even need some help.'

'No problem,' Quinn quickly assured her. 'I happen to know a wonderful little bridal boutique in Seattle . . . '

THE END

We do hope that you have enjoyed reading this large print book.

Did you know that all of our titles are available for purchase?

We publish a wide range of high quality large print books including:
Romances, Mysteries, Classics
General Fiction
Non Fiction and Westerns

Special interest titles available in large print are:
The Little Oxford Dictionary
Music Book, Song Book
Hymn Book, Service Book

Also available from us courtesy of Oxford University Press:
Young Readers' Dictionary
(large print edition)
Young Readers' Thesaurus
(large print edition)

For further information or a free brochure, please contact us at:
Ulverscroft Large Print Books Ltd.,
The Green, Bradgate Road, Anstey,
Leicester, LE7 7FU, England.
Tel: (00 44) **0116 236 4325**
Fax: (00 44) **0116 234 0205**

HEALING LOVE

Cara Cooper

Dr James Frayne's personal life is in meltdown and it is beginning to affect his work. Becky, his Practice Manager, is deeply concerned and wants to help. But Dr James cannot afford to let her in on his secret — if she discovers what's troubling him, it could lose him his job. When his cold efficiency and her powers of deduction collide, sparks fly and emotions are stirred — changing both their lives forever . . .

ANGEL HARVEST

Glenis Wilson

Jennifer Dunbar's dream of becoming a successful lady jockey seems to be over when she has to quit to look after Ellie, her three-year-old niece. Ellie's mother, Rosamund, was killed during a thunderstorm. Mystery surrounds her death — and the identity of Ellie's father. Jennifer is determined to find him. But her search impacts upon other people, threatening to destroy not only their lives, but also her own. Then Jennifer discovers — too late — some secrets should remain secret . . .

FORTUNES OF WAR

Jasmina Svenne

Since being orphaned, Lucy Prior has led a quiet life with her brother and his family on their farm in upstate New York. Now though, that peaceful existence is threatened by the approach of the American War of Independence. Even so, when she stumbles upon a handsome stranger hiding in the byre, Lucy cannot resist shielding him from his pursuers. But her actions will have far-reaching consequences — not only for herself, but also for the whole of her family.

AT THE END OF THE RAINBOW

Wendy Kremer

Alex is escaping from an unhappy love affair. She finds employment helping Julian to finish writing his latest book. Julian is partially paralysed, and confined to a wheelchair — the result of a car accident in which his wife was killed. He could improve — perhaps even restore — his mobility by accepting new medical treatment. But he goes on punishing himself. Can Alex and Julian forget the past, and find a future together?